D0542151

INTERIOR
CHINATOWN

Charles Yu

INTERIOR CHINATOWN

Europa
editions

Europa Editions
8 Blackstock Mews
London N4 2BT
www.europaeditions.co.uk

A catalogue record for this title is available from the British Library
ISBN 978-1-78770-257-8

Yu, Charles
Interior Chinatown

Book design and cover illustration by Emanuele Ragnisco
www.mekkanografici.com

Prepress by Grafica Punto Print – Rome

Printed and bound in Great Britain by Clays Ltd, Elcograf S.p.A.

CONTENTS

For Sophia and Dylan

INTERIOR
CHINATOWN

If a film needed an exotic
backdrop . . . Chinatown
could be made to represent
itself or any other
Chinatown in the world.
Even today, it stands in
for the ambiguous Asian
anywhere.

                    -Bonnie Tsui

ACT I
GENERIC ASIAN MAN

INT. GOLDEN PALACE

Ever since you were a boy, you've dreamt of being Kung Fu Guy.

You are not Kung Fu Guy.

You are currently Background Oriental Male, but you've been practicing.

Maybe tomorrow will be the day.

INT. GOLDEN PALACE

Ever since you were a boy, you've dreamt of being Kung Fu Guy.

You are not Kung Fu Guy.

You are currently Background Oriental Male, but you've been practicing.

Maybe tomorrow will be the day.

Take what you
can get.

Try to build
a life.

A life
at the
margin

made from
bit parts.

WILLIS WU
(ASIAN) ACTOR

Skills:

Kung Fu (Moderate Proficiency)
Fluent in Accented English
Able to do Face of Great Shame on command

Résumé/Repertoire:

Disgraced Son
Delivery Guy
Silent Henchman
Caught Between Two Worlds
Guy Who Runs in and Gets Kicked in the Face
Striving Immigrant
Generic Asian Man

Your mother has played, in no particular order:

Pretty Oriental Flower
Asiatic Seductress
Young Dragon Lady
Slightly Less Young Dragon Lady
Restaurant Hostess
Girl with the Almond Eyes
Beautiful Maiden Number One
Dead Beautiful Maiden Number One
Old Asian Woman

Your father has been, at various times:

Twin Dragon
Wizened Chinaman
Guy in a Soiled T-shirt
Inscrutable Grocery Owner (in a Soiled
T-shirt)
Egg Roll Cook
Young Asian Man
Sifu, the Mysterious Kung Fu Master
Old Asian Man

INT. GOLDEN PALACE—MORNING

In the world of Black and White, everyone
starts out as Generic Asian Man. Everyone who
looks like you, anyway. Unless you're a woman,
in which case you start out as Pretty Asian
Woman.

You all work at Golden Palace, formerly
Jade Palace, formerly Palace of Good Fortune.
There's an aquarium in the front and cloudy
tanks of rock crabs and two-pound lobsters
crawling over each other in the back.
Laminated menus offer the lunch special, which
comes with a bowl of fluffy white rice and
choice of soup, egg drop or hot and sour. A
neon Tsingtao sign blinks and buzzes behind
the bar in the dimly lit space, a dropped-
ceiling room with lacquered ornate woodwork
(or some imitation thereof), everything
simmering in a warm, seedy red glow thrown off
by the dollar-store paper lanterns festooned
above, many of them darkened by dead moths,
the paper yellowing, ripped, curling in on
itself.

The bar is fully stocked with top-shelf
spirits up top, middle-shelf liquor at eye
level, and down at the bottom, a happy hour
shelf of booze that you will regret for sure.
The new thing everyone is excited about is
called the lychee margarita-tini, which seems
like a lot of flavors. Not that you've had
one. They're fourteen bucks. Sometimes patrons
leave a sip at the bottom of the glass and if
you're quick, while you go through the

swinging door that separates the front of the house from the back, you can have a taste—you've seen some of the other Generic Asian Men do it. It's a risk, though. The director's always got an eye out, ready to fire someone for the smallest infraction.

You wear the uniform: white shirt, black pants. Black slipperlike shoes that have no traction whatsoever. Your haircut is not good, to say the least.

Black and White always look good. A lot of it has to do with the light. They're the heroes. They get hero lighting, designed to hit their faces just right. Designed to hit White's face just right, anyway.

Someday you want the light to hit your face like that. To look like the hero. Or for a moment to actually be the hero.

ROLES

First, you have to work your way up. Starting from the bottom, it goes:
5. Background Oriental Male
4. Dead Asian Man
3. Generic Asian Man Number Three/ Delivery Guy
2. Generic Asian Man Number Two/Waiter
1. Generic Asian Man Number One

and then if you make it that far (hardly anyone does) you get stuck at Number One for a while and hope and pray for the light to find

you and that when it does you'll have
something to say and when you say that
something it will come out just right and have
everyone in Black and White turning their
heads saying wow who is that, that is not just
some Generic Asian Man, that is a star, maybe
not a real, regular star, let's not get crazy,
we're talking about Chinatown here, but
perhaps a Very Special Guest Star, which for
your people is the ceiling, is the terminal,
ultimate, exalted position for any Asian
working in this world, the thing every
Oriental Male dreams of when he's in the
Background, trying to blend in.

Kung Fu Guy.

Kung Fu Guy is not like the other slots in
the hierarchy—there isn't always someone
occupying the position, as in whoever the top
guy is at any given time, that's the default
guy who gets trotted out whenever there's kung
fu to be done. Only a very special Asian can
be worthy of the title. It takes years of
dedication and sacrifice, and after all that
only a few have even a slim chance of making
it. Despite the odds, you all grew up training
for this and only this. All the scrawny yellow
boys up and down the block dreaming the same
dream.

INT. GOLDEN PALACE

Ever since you were a boy, you've dreamt of being Kung Fu Guy.

You are still not Kung Fu Guy.

You are currently Generic Asian Man Number Three/Delivery Guy. Your kung fu is B, B-plus on a good day, and Sifu once proclaimed your drunken monkey to be nearly at a level of competence that he could perhaps at some point in the future imagine not being completely embarrassed of you. Which, if you know him, well, that's a pretty big deal.

To be honest though it can sometimes be hard to tell with Sifu, who is famously inscrutable. If you could only show him what you've become. All you want is for him to make that face, the one that looks like internal distress possibly of a gastrointestinal nature but actually indicates something closer to Deeply Repressed Secret Pride Honorable Father Has for His Young but Promising Son; means Deliciously Bittersweet Pain That Comes from Knowing Honorable Teacher Is No Longer Needed. That's how you see it in your head: he would make that face, smile, you'd smile back. Credits roll and you'd walk off, arm in arm, to the horizon.

OLD ASIAN MAN

These days he is mostly Old Asian Man. No
longer Sifu, with the pants and the muscles
and the look in his eye. All of that is gone
now, but when did it happen? Over years and
overnight.

The day you first noticed. You'd shown up a
few minutes early for weekly lesson. Maybe
that's what threw him off. When he answered
the door, it took him a moment to recognize
you. Two seconds, or twenty, a frozen
eternity—then, as he regained himself, his
familiar scowl, barking your name

WILLIS WU!

half-exclamation, half-confirmation, as if
verifying for both you and himself that he
hadn't forgotten. Willis Wu, he said again,
well come on, what are you doing, don't just
stand there in the doorway like a dum-dum,
come in, son, let's get started.

He was fine for the rest of the day,
mostly, but you couldn't stop thinking about
the look he gave you, oblivion or terror, and
for the first time you noticed the mess his
room had become, not unusual for any other man
his age living alone, but for Sifu, who taught
and valued order and simplicity in all things,
to have allowed his dwelling to reach this
state of disorganization should have been a
warning sign to all. Maybe not the first, but
the first one that came to your attention.

Fatty Choy went around telling everyone that Sifu was on food stamps, saying how gullible can you be ("You idiots think being Wizened Chinaman pays well? Are you crazy? Why do you think he fishes bottles and cans out of the trash?") but no one wanted to believe it. At least in public. In private, the thought did occur. Sifu never had the lights on. Said it was to train the senses. He saved everything: disposable chopsticks, free glossy calendars from East-West Bank ("good for wrapping fish or fruit"), packets of soy sauce and chili paste from the dollar Chinese down the street. He'd patched his old fake leather couch so many times there were cracks on the patches. Which of course he also patched. The Formica two-top he ate on was the first and only kitchen table he'd ever bought, purchased for seven dollars and fifty cents from the salvage bin at the old restaurant supply warehouse down on Jackson and Eighth, that place long gone now (converted to INT. RAVE/ GRIMY CLUB SCENE) but the table still there in the kitchen. An artifact of the previous century, it had worn down to a smoothness so comforting and cool it felt soft to the touch, the patterns of use, hundreds, thousands of meals together in the corner of that small, low-ceilinged room, the surface preserving the teachings of Sifu, wisdom over time recorded in the warp and wear, in the markings of the modest table itself. Come to think of it, Fatty Choy, despite the fact that he was and had always been a total gasbag, a mostly insufferable close-talking blowhard (made all the more insufferable by the fact that he was not infrequently right about things), was simply stating what you all knew but didn't want to admit: Sifu had gotten old.

It was easy to lie to yourself about it. Although naively you believed he had by some miracle of genetics and sheer follicular willpower managed to reach his seventh decade without a single hair turning gray, in hindsight you remember once seeing an empty box of natural seaweed coloring in his wastebasket, Sifu emerging from his room with the occasional smear where he'd gotten a little careless and ended up painting the top edge of his forehead a swath of kelpish green.

And even if he could still break a cinder block with three fingers, that was nothing compared to back in the day, his younger self, when he could do it with just one—a single powerful blow of any digit. You pick! You couldn't bear to watch, peeking through your fingers when you were little, and as you got older still wincing in expectation of painful failure. But young Sifu never failed. He always found the necessary reserves of qi, was able to summon forth from whatever intangible reservoir the required force to smash through it, and everyone gathered around would clap and shout their praise at the latest demonstration of Sifu's mind over matter, mental and physical, an impossible feat right there in the alley behind the kitchen in the middle of a Tuesday. At the sound of the

exploding energy you would uncover your eyes
and exhale with relief, proud and grateful
that he had done it once again, hadn't mangled
his hand, and also slightly ashamed by your
lack of faith, when everyone else, the
assembled friends and strangers, had never
doubted him in the slightest.

Your earliest memories of him as a young
dragon, a rising star, thick straight hair the
color of night combed slowly and carefully
straight back in a lustrous wave. Forearms
like steel barrels lifting you out of the
makeshift playpen in the corner of the room
and flying you around up above his head,
almost crashing into the bed and the lamp and
the ceiling as you laughed and laughed until
your mother said *sio sim, sio sim,* that's
enough, Ming, please, stop before he gets
sick, and he'd do one more revolution before
setting you down safely, your feet back on
solid ground, the world still spinning.

Whether we admitted to it or not, and
sometimes you did admit it to yourself, right
before falling asleep, in the way thoughts
like this come to you: your first, best, and
only real master, the source of all your kung
fu knowledge, was no longer himself. He'd aged
out of his role and into the next one, his
life force depleting with every exertion.
Wisdom and power leaking from him with each
passing day and night. He'd played his role
for so long he'd lost himself in it, before
some separation that happened gradually over
decades, and then you waking one day to feel

it, some distance that had crept in overnight. Some formal space you could no longer cross.

He'd always be Your Father, but somehow was no longer your dad.

No longer running up walls, no more leaping from the curved roof eaves of the Bank of America pagoda. More often found nodding off during a meal, eaten alone, in front of the six o'clock news. Long after you'd graduated into an adult role, you still continued coming to him for these weekly lessons, but the lessons had turned into a flimsy pretense layered atop their real purpose: your delivery of provisions on which your old man depended. A few groceries, toilet paper, his various prescriptions. Putting things out so they'd be easy for him to access, wiping the floor as best you could. There was only so much time. Checking for dampness on his mattress pad, changing it if necessary, picking up laundry, sweeping from his nightstand the accumulation of balled-up napkins enclosing clots of dried phlegm and blood. More napkins behind the nightstand and all around, a half-eaten pear under the Formica table, there since the day after your last visit, having dropped and rolled to a stop right in that very spot, left to slowly rot, the gentle descent into squalor not a function of sloth but simple, physical inability.

I'm sorry. I can't reach.

It's okay, Ba. I got it.

The apologies, the true sign—that this was not the man you once knew, a man who would never have uttered that word to his son, sorry, and in English, no less. Not because he thought himself infallible, but because of his belief that a family should never have to say sorry, or please, or thank you, for that matter, these things being redundant, being contradictory to the parent-son relationship, needing to remain unstated always, these things being the invisible fabric of what a family is.

You did what you could despite being generally ignored. Sifu-now-Old-Asian-Man having forgotten not just his kung fu technique but also his most loyal student, regarding you with a blank if slightly wary amiability, as one might endure an overbearing but helpful stranger. Your relationship having turned into a pantomime, a series of gestures in a well-worn scene, played out again and again, any underlying feeling having long since been obviated by emotional muscle memory, learning how to make the right faces, strike the right poses, not out of apathy or lack of sincerity, rather a need to preserve what was left of his pride.

The trick was learning what not to say. To enter the theater of his dotage quietly, sit there in the dark and not ask him any question, however simple, that might cause momentary confusion, might turn your rote interactions into something too raw, remind yourselves or each other of what was happening here, the inversion of the relationship, the care and feeding, the brute fact of physical dependency: If you don't do this, he can't do it for himself. If you miss a week, he sits in the dark. Not that he'll die. Although there is always that possibility. But he'll be lonelier that day, hungrier. He'll lose something or drop something or break something and have to wait for you to call or come by. Staying in character avoided all of that, allowed you to prolong your respective roles for just a bit longer, and in a good week, when things were going along relatively well, you could get by, could walk through your blocking and lines, make it to the end of the day. But on bad days or if you'd stay too long, his patience or working memory would reach its limit, and he'd edge into a twilight distrust, fear in his eyes.

Even on the worst days, he never completely forgot you for more than a minute or two—somehow in his paranoia you sensed he always knew that you were *someone* to him. You suspect that only made him more afraid of you, your presence a vague familiarity triggering in some deep part of his memory an inchoate, low-level anxiety, the son returning home, the lost son come to assert his right to challenge the father.

In the months since, he eventually settled into a new, diminished equilibrium, even began to work again, as Old Asian Cook or Old Asian Guy Smoking, which was rough, was a hard thing to see for anyone who'd known him back when. Known what he'd been capable of. A new role, a new phase of life, it could be a way of starting fresh, the slate wiped clean.

But the old parts are always underneath. Layers upon layers, accumulating. Which was the problem. No one in Chinatown able to separate the past from the present, always seeing in him (and in each other, in yourselves) all of his former incarnations, the characters he'd played in your minds long after the parts had ended.

In that way, Sifu had gotten this old without anyone noticing. Including your mother—deemed to have aged out of Asian Seductress, no longer Girl with the Almond Eyes, now Old Asian Woman—living down the hall, their marriage having entered its own dusky phase, bound for eternity but separate in life. The rationale being that she needed to continue to work in order to be able to support him and for that she needed a minimum amount of rest and peace of mind, all true, and that they were better apart than together, also true. The reality being that they'd lost the plot somewhere along the way, their once great romance spun into a period piece, into an immigrant family story, and then into a story about two people trying to get by. And it was just that: getting by. Barely, and no more. Because they'd also, in the way old people often do, slipped gently into poverty. Also without anyone noticing.

Poor is relative, of course. None of you were rich or had any dreams of being rich or even knew anyone rich. But the widest gulf in the world is the distance between getting by and not quite getting by. Crossing that gap

can happen in a hundred ways, almost all by
accident. Bad day at work and/or kid has a
fever and/or miss the bus and consequently ten
minutes late to the audition which equals you
don't get to play the part of Background
Oriental with Downtrodden Face. Which equals,
stretch the dollar that week, boil chicken bones
twice for a watery soup, make the bottom of the
bag of rice last another dinner or three.

Cross that gap and everything changes.
Being on this side of it means that time
becomes your enemy. You don't grind the day—
the day grinds you. With the passing of every
month your embarrassment compounds,
accumulates with the inevitability of a simple
arithmetic truth. X is less than Y, and
there's nothing to be done about that. The
daily mail bringing with it fresh dread or
relief, but if the latter, only the most
temporary kind, restarting the clock on the
countdown to the next bill or past-due notice
or collection agency call.

Sifu, like many others INT. CHINATOWN SRO,
had without warning or complaint slid just
under the line so quietly, it was easy to
minimize how painful it must have been. The
pain of having once been young, with muscles,
still able to work. To have lived an entire
life of productivity, of self-sufficiency,
having been a net giver, never a taker, never
relying on others. To call oneself master, to
hold oneself out as a source of expertise, to
have had the courage and ability and
discipline that added up to a meaningful,

perhaps even noteworthy life, built over decades from nothing, and then at some point in that serious life, finding oneself searching for *calories*. Knowing what time of day the restaurant tosses its leftover steamed pork buns. Not in a position to turn down any food, however obtained, eyeing the markdown bins in the ninety-nine-cent store, full of dense, sugary bricks and slabs and disk-sized cookies, not food really, really only meant for children, something to fill the belly of a person who once took himself seriously. Buying this food without hesitation, necessity overcoming any shame in simply eating it, and not just eating it, swallowing it down more quickly than intended, a young man's dignity replaced by a newly acquired clumsiness, the hands and mouth and belly knowing what the heart and head had not yet come to terms with: hunger. Nothing like an empty stomach to remind you what you are.

To be fair, it wasn't as if anyone in Chinatown was in a great monetary position to be helping Sifu. Old Asian Woman did what she could, but as work slowed down, had enough of a challenge trying to take care of herself. And you just starting out, contributing what you could manage, a bag of food or medicine, once in a while a piece of fish or meat. That's what you tell yourself anyway. The truth being that if each of you had done a little, together it might have been enough.

OLDER BROTHER

Some say that the person who should have helped the most, was in a position to help the most, having been Sifu's number-one-most-naturally-gifted-kung-fu-superstar-in-training-pupil all those years and thus having reaped the greatest benefit from Sifu's teachings, was Older Brother.

Not your actual older brother. Better. Everyone's Older Brother. The prodigy. The homecoming king. Unofficial mayor of the neighborhood. Guardian of Chinatown.

Once the heir apparent to Sifu, the two of them even starring together in a brief but notable project about father-and-son martial arts experts (Logline: When political considerations make conventional military tactics impossible, the government calls on a highly secretive elite special ops force—a father-son duo among the best hand-to-hand fighters in the world—in order to get the job done, Codename: TWIN DRAGONS).

Older Brother, who never had to work his way up the ladder, never had to be Generic Asian Man. Older Brother, who was born, bred, and trained to be, and eventually did become, Kung Fu Guy, which meant, of course, making Kung Fu Guy money, which is good for your kind but still basically falls under the general category of secondary roles.

Older Brother.

Like Bruce Lee, but also completely different.

Lee being legendary, not mythical. Too real, too specific to be a myth, the particulars of his genius known and part of his ever-accumulating personal lore. Electromuscular stimulation. Ingesting huge quantities of royal jelly. And with his development of his own discipline, Jeet Kune Do, the creation of an entirely new fighting system and philosophical worldview. Bruce Lee was proof: not all Asian Men were doomed to a life of being Generic. If there was even one guy who had made it, it was at least theoretically possible for the rest.

But easy cases make bad law, and Bruce Lee proved too much. He was a living, breathing video game boss-level, a human cheat code, an idealized avatar of Asian-ness and awesomeness permanently set on Expert difficulty. Not a man so much as a personification, not a mortal so much as a deity on loan to you and your kind for a fixed period of time. A flame that burned for all yellow to understand, however briefly, what perfection was like.

Older Brother was the inverse.

Not a legend but a myth.

Or a whole bunch of myths, overlapping, redundant, contradictory. A mosaic of ideas, a thousand and one puzzle pieces that teased you, let you see the edges of something, clusters here and there, just enough to keep hope alive that the next piece would be the one, the answer snapping into place, showing how it all fit together.

Bruce Lee was the guy you worshipped. Older

Brother was the guy you dreamt of growing up to be.

BEGIN OLDER BROTHER AWESOMENESS MONTAGE:

—Older Brother always has the good hair, not the kind that goes straight up and then out at weird angles and with stupid cowlicks in the back and on the side and wherever else. Not the kind that makes you think of math club and pocket protectors. Older Brother was blessed, among other things, with the rare phenotype, the kind of Asian dude hair with a slight wave to it (but always in a tight fade), thick and black but with brown or even red highlights.

—Older Brother's kung fu is A-plus-plus, obviously, but he isn't limited to just kung fu. He can also mess around with Muay Thai, is proficient in a couple forms of judo, and is definitely down with Taekwondo (and its many strip mall variations). His Brazilian grappling is legit if you care to go to ground with him, but you shouldn't because in about eight seconds you'll be tapping the mat, asking him through tears of excruciating pain to please stop bending your arm that way.

—If you get Older Brother drunk enough (not that he ever really gets drunk, just sort of slightly faded, Older Brother's legendary tolerance for alcohol having been proven time and again in countless drinking games and late-night wagers, some fun, some not so fun) he will show you knife tricks that will leave you laughing and scared shitless at the same time and he will do it effortlessly, knife in one hand, beer in the other, his long hair looking cool.

—It's not clear if he can dunk (no one's ever seen him try) but he can definitely grab the rim and that alone is pretty impressive given that he's five eleven and three-quarters.

—Which, for the record, is the perfect height for an Asian dude. Tall enough for women to notice (even in heels! even White women!), tall enough to not get ignored by the bartender, but not so tall to get called Yao Ming and considered some kind of Mongolian freak.

—And if you get any ideas that you could take him in a bar fight or on the basketball court or anywhere else, you'll quickly find out the hard way what a bad idea that is. Guys don't want to fight him anyway—they call him Bruce ("Yo, yo, I've seen *Fists of Fury* like a hundred times"), or Jackie or Jet Li, and he's cool with it all, whatever the vibe, wherever it's coming from. Everyone admired his level of comfort, moving in and out of language and subculture, from backroom poker games to dudes on the corner looking for trouble to the octogenarians playing Go or mahjong at the Benevolent Family Association. Older Brother's reach and influence was not limited to the Middle Kingdom and its ethnic diaspora, but extended into other neighboring domains: he could sing karaoke with the Japanese salarymen, could polish off two plates of ddukbokki slathered in a tangy, blood-red gochujang, wash it down with a bottle of milky soju, all while beating the pants off the K-town regulars at their own drinking games, dropping some of his passable Korean (mostly curse words) in the process.

—Older Brother was never in a gang, not even close, makes a point of not even being loosely affiliated with a triad or Wah Ching, yet somehow manages it so that those scary dudes are still cool with him. He gives them their distance and they do the same with him, a form of silent respect.

—On top of all this, Older Brother was a National Merit Scholar. 1570 on the SAT.

—Everyone has their own story about Older Brother.

"Man you don't even know. Last week I saw him at Jackson and Eleventh."
"What was he doing?"
"Chin-ups on the cross bar of the traffic signal."
"I saw him, too."
"No you didn't."
"I did. He was doing them one-handed."

"No shit one-handed. OB doesn't mess around with regular chin-ups. Not like your weak sauce."

"You're weak sauce."

"Say that again. To my face."

"You're weak sauce."

"Shut up, idiots. Did one of you really see Older Brother?"

"Yeah. Like I said. Chin-ups. Did like fifty of them."

"More like seventy."

"With his left hand."

"He's left-handed, dumbass."

"Older Brother is left-handed? Come on. You're the dumbass, dumbass."

"He's ambidextrous. You're both dumbasses."

—That's pretty much how it goes with Older Brother stories piled on more stories, conflicting, combining, canceling each other out. In the end, you're not sure how much of it's real and how much is local lore, exploits that over the years have expanded, but in any case it doesn't matter. Even if Older Brother were not actually a real person, he would still be the most important character in some yet-to-be-conceived-story of Chinatown. Would still be real in everyone's minds and hearts, the mythical Asian American man, the ideal mix of assimilated and authentic. Plus, the bonus: a viable romantic lead. Older Brother is the guy who makes every kid in Chinatown want to be better, taller, stronger, faster, more mainstream and somehow less at the same time.

Makes every one of you want to be cooler than you're supposed to be, than you're allowed to be. Gives you permission to try.

—For a brief period during Older Brother's ascendancy, all felt right. What was happening was what was meant to happen. The chosen one, the best and brightest and most conventionally-handsome-by-Western-standards, he had worked his way up in the system, had reached his designated station of maximal achievement. All other Asian Men stood in his shadow, feeling anything was possible or, if not anything then at least something. Something was possible. You put your heads on pillows at night and went to sleep dreaming of what it would look like, to be part of the show, lie awake wondering how much higher Older Brother might rise within Black and White. What that would mean for the rest of you.

—And then you woke up one morning and it was over. The dream had ended. Older Brother was no longer Kung Fu Guy. The details secret, the official story that it just didn't work out. The upshot for all of you was: no more Kung Fu Guy. Somehow, the golden era of Older Brother was over, without warning or fanfare or any kind of reason, really. Or at least, no official reason. Unofficially, we understood. There was a ceiling. Always had been, always would be. Even for him. Even for our hero, there were limits to the dream of assimilation, to how far any of you could make your way into the world of Black and White.

It was probably for the best. For him, personally anyway. Older Brother, despite all of his success, never seemed entirely comfortable with his preordained place in the hierarchy, was never totally down with the whole career track. Didn't see himself as a Kung Fu Guy. And he wasn't wrong. His kung fu was too pure, too special to be used the way that everyone knew it would be: flashy, stupid shit, the same moves everyone had seen a million times and yet still wanted him to trot out for every wedding and lunar new year celebration. Better that fame had never happened on him, to preserve his claim for posterity. Better to be a legend than a star.

END OLDER BROTHER AWESOMENESS MONTAGE

A performer may be taken in by his own act, convinced at the moment that the impression of reality which he fosters is the one and only reality. In such cases we have a sense in which the performer comes to be his own audience; he comes to be the performer and observer of the same show.

Erving Goffman

ACT II
INT. GOLDEN PALACE

SHE'S

the most accomplished young detective
in the history of the department.

HE'S

a third-generation cop who left Wall Street to
honor his father's legacy.

<u>TOGETHER</u>

they head the Impossible Crimes Unit, tasked
with cracking the most unsolvable cases.

When all others have failed, the ICU is the
last hope for <u>justice</u>.

When all others have failed, you call:

<u>BLACK AND WHITE</u>

This is their story.

INT. GOLDEN PALACE CHINESE RESTAURANT—NIGHT

Dead Asian Guy is dead.

                    WHITE LADY COP
          He's dead.

                    BLACK DUDE COP
          Looks that way.

Our heroes regard the prone Asian male body,
partially covered with a sheet.

                    BLACK DUDE COP
          Next of kin?

                    WHITE LADY COP
          Checking.

A crime scene investigator swabs something.
Another measures the radius and dispersal
pattern of a pool of drying blood. A female
officer in uniform (BLACK, 20S, ATTRACTIVE)
approaches White Lady Cop and Black Dude
Cop.

                    BLACK DUDE COP
          Whaddya got?

                    ATTRACTIVE OFFICER
          Restaurant worker says the parents
          live nearby. We're hunting down an
          address.

                    WHITE LADY COP
          Good. We'll pay a visit. Might have
          some questions for them.
             (then)
          Anyone else?

                    ATTRACTIVE OFFICER
          A brother.
          Seems to have gone missing.

Black and White exchange a look.

                    BLACK DUDE COP
          This might be a case of—

                    WHITE LADY COP
          The Wong guy.

White: deadpan. Black tries hard but like
always, he breaks first, flashing his
trademark smile. White holds steady a beat
longer but then she breaks, too. It's their
show and they have the comfort of knowing it
can't go on without them.
    "Sorry sorry. I'm so sorry," White says,
trying to keep it together. "Can we do that
again?" They've managed to stop laughing when
Black's nose makes a snort and sends them back
into another round of giggles.

BLACK AND WHITE. Two cops, one of each race.
In the opening credits they drive around in a
black-and-white police car, even though
they're detectives. Which doesn't make sense.

Often neither does the plot nor the motivations of the characters, nor the backstory, nor any of it, if you think too hard, which means thinking about it for more than the time spent watching it. But the template works, and you don't mess with a working template.

Sometimes there's a Floating Latina. They put her on marketing materials in select demographically targeted neighborhoods. Technically on the poster, but not where your eye lands. She's off to the side, her head near the edge, smaller than those of Black and White (and thus, through the magic of forced perspective, rendered a good ways behind the two leads). Her pretty face hovering in a sea of abstract space.

There's a pattern, a form, a certain shape to it all. The idea that any problem, no matter how messy and blood-spattered, from EXT. STREET TO INT. OFFICE or INT. CRIME LAB OR INT. CHINESE RESTAURANT, any blight or societal ill, any crime of hate or intolerance, can be wrapped into the template. The idea that there are clues, and the clues can be discovered and understood, at a reasonable pace, i.e., one major breakthrough or setback for every commercial break, with each act a new understanding of the problem. That they, our heroes, can get to the bottom of things, and in the end, it's human nature (jealousy and treachery and, you know, murder). A strangely optimistic idea. A deeply ingrained hope that they, Black and White, will be able to face that danger, get a handle on it. Downtown may be gritty and dark and full of evil but on some level an unspoken belief, a faith that we live in a manageable world with its own episodic rules and conventions:

Life takes place one hour at a time.

Clues present themselves in order, one at a time.

Two investigators, properly paired, can solve any mystery.

And there's just something about Asians—their faces, their skin color—it just automatically takes you out of this reality. Forces you to step back and say, *Whoa, whoa, what is this? What kind of world are we in? And what are these Asians doing in my cop show?*

There's just something about Asians that makes reality a little too real, overcomplicates the clarity, the duality, the clean elegance of BLACK and WHITE, the proven template and so the decision is made not in some overarching conspiracy to exclude Asians but because it's just easier to keep it how we have it. Two cops roaming the city. The precinct, the car, the bar after work. The decision is made but it's not a decision at all, it's the opposite. It's the way things are. You do the cop show. You get your little check. You wonder: Can you change it? Can you be the one who actually breaks through?

INT. GOLDEN PALACE CHINESE RESTAURANT—TAKE TWO

Dead Asian Guy, still dead.

                  WHITE LADY COP
    He's dead.

                  BLACK DUDE COP
    Mmhmm.

                  WHITE LADY COP
    So we have a body.

                  BLACK DUDE COP
    We have a body.

CLOSE ON: White Lady Cop.

SARAH GREEN, 31

pretty but tough but emphasis on the pretty.
Smart cookie. Good at her job. Great at her
job. Came from a broken home, worked her way
up to become the most respected detective on
the force. Hair pulled back in a ponytail,
suggesting general competence with the
handling of her weapon and herself and also
that she's the kind of gal that orders draft
beer if it's available and is not averse to
glancing at the sports section if it happens
to be lying around. That kind of gal. Also,
pretty. In case that wasn't clear already.
Very very pretty.

                    GREEN
          (gazing at a dead Chinaman)
      What are we looking at?

                 BLACK DUDE COP
        Family drama, probably.
            (pause for effect; chimes in the
            distance, vaguely Oriental)
        Some kind of cultural thing.

CLOSE ON: Black Dude Cop.

MILES TURNER, 33.

Tall and built. Really built. Like, if-gray-T-
shirts-hadn't-been-invented-already-they-
would-have-to-be-invented-just-so-Miles-could-
wear-the-shit-out-of-them built. That kind of
built.

Fade tight, edges perfect, skin flawless.
Distractingly handsome. Yale then Goldman then
a hedge fund, on his way to even bigger things
when his father, twenty-seven-year veteran of
the NYPD, was killed in the line of duty.
Entered the academy the day after his dad's
funeral, graduated top of his class. Been on
the force ever since—going on eleven years
now, but starting to get antsy.

Youngest in department history to ever make
detective (recruited by the FBI, as well as
several NYC billionaires to head private
security). Cops don't usually get this famous,
but then again Miles Turner is no ordinary
cop. Everyone wants a piece of him. Currently

weighing his options, but can't bring himself
to tell Green yet. They're a team—and,
considering the smoldering looks—maybe
something more?

                    TURNER
               (sexy whisper)
          You hear something?

                              You're off to the
                              side watching all of
                              this. A spectator.

Black and White both turn to look offscreen,
peering into the darkness, their faces lit
perfectly. But there's nothing there. Then:

                    GREEN
          Miles.

                    TURNER
          What?

A sound, from deep background, in the
alleyway—richly audible sound effects.

In the shadows is OLD ASIAN MAN, 70s.

Turner draws his weapon, steady and calm.
Green draws her piece as well, flicks the
safety off, finger on the trigger. She looks
uncharacteristically nervous.

                    TURNER
        Who's there?

                    GREEN
        Hands where we can see them.

                              They're going to
                        shoot him. You have
                            to say something.
                        But how can you? You
                        don't have any lines.

Old Asian Man steps into the light. Turner
sees him just in time.

                    TURNER
            No!

Green lowers her weapon, breathing heavily.
Turner clenches his jaw.

                    GREEN
        Thank you, Miles.

They share a meaningful look—this is the heart
of Black and White, right here, how their
partnership evolves, and of course, all this
sexy eye contact.
    In front of them is the person Green almost
shot: Old Asian Man, pushing a cart full of
plastic bottles.
    Turner shifts his weight, nervous.

GREEN

Sir?

TURNER
(to Green)
I don't think he understands you.

Turner turns toward Old Asian Man, stoops down a little.

TURNER (CONT'D)
(little too loud)
Do you understand me?

OLD ASIAN MAN
(without accent)
Yeah, man. I speak English.

Old Asian Man turns to you and smiles.
Green laughs. Turner, pissed, looks at the director.
The director yells CUT.

Ever since you were a boy, you've dreamt of being Kung Fu Guy.

You're not Kung Fu Guy.

But maybe, just maybe, tomorrow will be the day.

INT. CHINATOWN SRO

Home is a room on the eighth floor of the
Chinatown SRO Apartments. Open a window in the
SRO on a summer night and you can hear at
least five dialects being spoken, the voices
bouncing up and down the central interior
courtyard, the courtyard in reality just a
vertical column of interior-facing windows,
also serving as the community clothes drying
space, crisscrossing lines of kung fu pants
for all the Generic Asian Men, and for the
Nameless Asian Women, cheap knockoff qipaos,
slit high up the thigh, or a bit more modest
for Matronly Asian Ladies, terrycloth bibs for
Undernourished Asian Babies, often shown in
montages, and of course don't forget the
granny panties and soiled A-shirts for Old
Asian Women and Old Asian Men, respectively.
This interior space also acting as a conduit
for information via the invisible, complex,
and (to an outsider) incomprehensible inter-
window messaging system for the building,
which works in real time and is lower than the
lowest of tech—basically you point your face
in the general direction of the person you
want to communicate with and you yell at them
what you want them to know. Somehow, despite
the cacophony (or because of it) your
recipient usually gets the message.
    In the long tradition of immigrants living
above their place of work, the SRO sits on top
of Golden Palace. It goes: ground floor
restaurant, the mezzanine for offices, then

seven more floors of SRO living—fifteen single-room apartments per floor, a small bathroom with shower and toilet at the end of the hall. Noises and odors from the kitchen never stop pushing up from below, day and night, year-round (even on Thanksgiving and Christmas), so that when you're sleeping you are, in a way, still inside the restaurant. You never really leave Golden Palace, even in your dreams.

INT. CHINATOWN SRO—STAIRWELL—NIGHT

As you climb the stairs to your room, you pass by every floor, each one its own ecosystem, its own set of rules and territories.

   The second floor is where your folks live. You should stop in. It would make her happy. Not that she would show it. Not that she would smile. More likely a scowl. You should be a better son. For a moment. But it won't be a moment. It'll be more. It will be guilt and that heavy feeling, it will be a deep sigh, it will be heavy and unspoken and you don't know if you can do that right now.

   The Cheuks live on three. Have lived in the SRO as long as your parents have. A daughter, who was smart, but ended up working downstairs, and a son, Tony Cheuk, who was luckier, was born a boy and had a chance to move to the city so he did, a good son who sent money and packages of food; when you were a kid, a Generic Asian Boy, you'd wander by their door, hoping to catch him on the right day and you might get lucky. Tony might give you an almond cookie from Phoenix Bakery or slip you a buck or two just to show off.

There's no fourth floor. Four is very bad. Four sounds like death.

Five is where the Hostess lives (20s, pretty, exotic)—she plays prostitutes so often the women here have shunned her, and the men and older boys hold doors open for her and say how can she be blamed for her beauty, while trying hard not to look too close, her skintight cheongsam hugging every curve. Also on five is the Casino, which is really just a room shared by three Asian Gangsters (late teens to mid-20s, tattoos, their stringy muscles and bony frames not quite filling out their crisp white undershirts; always smoking, even in their sleep).

Sixth floor is where the Monk lives—he hasn't spoken a word in forty years. Older Brother's room was down the hall from the Monk's. He was the only person the Monk would allow, their rooms on opposite ends of the floor.

On seven lives the Emperor. No kid is brave enough to knock on the Emperor's door. Legend has it that, many years ago, the Emperor played, well, an emperor. Ming Dynasty, imperial guards and everything (although by middle school most kids hear the full story, which is that the Emperor was the emperor as in Emperor's Delight, a brand of frozen Oriental Cuisine TV dinners—siu mai and har gow in just two minutes. Steamed buns in three. Just poke holes in the top with your fork, place in the microwave, and in no time you'll be ready to feast like the Emperor himself.

The Emperor's job was to present these plastic trays of steaming delicacies to a family of blond people somewhere in the middle of America, and then bow to them, while off-screen, in the shadows, a gong sounded (and further off-screen, in the mists of history, you could hear the collective weeping of a civilization going back five thousand years). Afterward, the Emperor would get his check and spend it on beer and rice liquor, tipping glass after glass until he was drunk enough to laugh about it, until he was drunk enough that he didn't feel shame or anything else, including his fingers and toes. Not that he had any need to be ashamed around the SRO. He had only admirers, and even today the Emperor has an imperial aura about him from that role, not to mention diminishing but non-negligible residuals supporting his claim to the throne. A few extra bucks a month goes a long way in this building.

On the eighth floor, you find your mother, standing near your door.

"Have you eaten?"

"What? How did you?"

"Elevator," she says.

"Ma. You know that thing is a death trap. No good thing has ever happened in that elevator."

"You were almost born in there."

"I'm not sure which way that goes."

"You didn't stop by," she says, and instantly your face turns hot.

You hug her and are reminded of how much she has shrunk in recent years, the top of her head maybe reaching your collarbone, if she stands up straight.

"Got some food for you," you say, handing her a plastic bag full of bah-chang.

"This is for me?"

"Yeah."

"You didn't drop it off," she says.

"I figured you'd come and get it eventually."

"Real nice, Willis," she says, but she takes it anyway. You see the scars on her sinewy wrist and forearm—twin belts of raised, darkened skin.

"There are a few different kinds in there. For Dad, too."

She looks in the bag.

"Yeah. The ones I like. With the mushrooms?" She smiles. "Go see your dad later," she says, more a request than a demand.

"How's he doing?"

"Not great. Could use your help."

"He won't talk to me. Not like he used to."

"Not that kind of help. He wants to move the bed over to the wall."

"He doesn't need me for that. The bed's not even—" But then you see the way she is looking at you and you realize: she wouldn't be asking if he could do it.

"Okay," you say. "I'll come down later."

FLASHBACK: YOUR MOTHER

The earliest memories you have of her, she is
Young Beautiful Oriental Woman.

She packs lunches for you, in her off-hours
costume: floral print blouse, polyester bellbottoms. She crouches by the narrow strip that
passes for counter space, assembling a small
pian-tong, a kid's lunch divided into neat
compartments: in the main section, three
boiled dumplings filled with ground pork and
bits of ginger and chopped-up scallions. In
the two smaller sections, a dollop of soft
rice with yam, and a handful of slightly
bruised grapes. She presses the lid down
tight, wraps a large rubber band around it for
good measure (you're five, you'll drop the box
at least three times before you eat), and
hands it to you.

You remember a hundred quiet dinners the
two of you had, your father still at work. For
dessert, more grapes or cubed cantaloupe if
you're lucky. If not, a Dixie cup of diluted
fruit-punch-flavored Hi-C. Room temperature
but you don't care. You sip carefully,
savoring each taste, and then when it's almost
gone, turn the cup all the way over until that
last stubborn drop makes its way down the waxy
inner surface onto your tongue. You take the
last bite of your dinner and announce that
you're done. I'm full, you say, but in truth

you want a little more and your mother knows it. She feeds you from her bowl. This close, you can smell her breath, sharp and almost sweet, vegetables and garlic. Telling you stories about how she first came to this country. Her dreams of what life would be here.

After dinner, she does the dishes in the communal sink down the hall, wipes them dry, and brings them back in the room, storing them under the table. (In an SRO you think in all three dimensions. A room isn't a layout, a footprint, it's a space, a volume, and when you start to understand that, you can't believe how much volume there is in here. You hang things, and you hang things on those things. You stack and pile and cram, you make use of every available cubic unit of your life, not just a floor plan or a schematic. You find hidden spaces within a hollow object, a hamper or a laundry basket, a box of dried tea leaves, a cookie tin, things inside things inside things.)

After she cleans herself up a bit, she goes downstairs to work at Golden Palace. She works nights, mostly, and the timing is off—her start time an hour or two before your dad gets home. You have a routine: you are allowed to watch television for thirty minutes after Ma leaves, and then you put yourself to bed.

You remember waiting by the front door as she put on her work costume. You remember the moment after she'd gone for the night. When it was quiet. Her emotional energy draining from

the room, her protective field slowly
dissipating.

FLASHBACK

Your mother studies from a textbook. *How to
Make $1,000,000 in Real Estate*. No experience
or capital needed, just a few basic principles
(location, location, location) and a
willingness to work hard.

The Friday nights she doesn't have work are
the best. A couple minutes to eight, you look
at her and she nods, and you click on the
television to the kung fu show. The opening
credits get your heart racing. The weary
traveler. The white dude that they dressed up
to look vaguely Asiatic. But you don't care.
You're here for the sound effects. You're here
for the martial arts.

The steady rhythm of foot strikes, hand
strikes, blows to the torso, blows to the
head. Then the music kicks in, jarring
dissonant strings, conflict in a minor key.
Random gongs.

Push in on our hero.

Push in on his opponent.

The eyes, it's in the eyes.

It's all too much, you can't resist, and
you're up, bouncing off the walls of the room,
your home, your world, a five-year-old. You
are a future Kung Fu Guy in training. Kung Fu
Kid.

                    KUNG FU KID
          Someday, I'm going to be Bruce Lee.

You repeat it, for effect.

                    KUNG FU KID
               (ahem)
          I said, someday, I'm going to be Bruce
          Lee.

And then one more time, but still no answer
from your mother, deeply engrossed in her
textbook. On-screen, two fighters
crisscrossing six feet above the ground,
somersaults in the air, butterfly kicks,
twisting horizontally, diagonally, three-
sixty, seventy-twenty, ten-eighty. Gravity
waiting patiently for the two black-haired
masters to succumb, not inevitably bound by
the rules of physics like regular mortals,
rather by choice, returning to earth only if
and when they feel like it and even then in
their own manner. Blue sky behind them, the
midday sun backlighting the whole scene in
such a way as to wash out all details—the
sweat on their temples, the features of their
chiseled, sinewy torsos—leaving only the
outlines, the stylized and timeless archetypes
of two masters being masterful. Hi-yah. Kung
Fu Kid leaps! Twists! Your leg slicing through
empty space, splitting the world in two. Wah.
Yah. Foom. Doing your own soundtrack. Gearing
up for the big move, full aerial splits, legs
horizontal, toes pointed, your lower body one

straight line, energy shooting from your feet
in both directions . . .

You pulled it off.

First time ever.

. . . Or so you thought, so close to
completing the move but then, as you land,
your foot catching the edge of a plastic tray
with your ma's pot of oolong steeping inside.
The tray now tracing out its own arc through
the air, everything in super-slow-mo, your
mother's face somehow remaining calm through
it all, the only flicker in her expression one
of momentary concern, as the pot of scalding
tea nearly hits you on its way down. She
catches it, or almost does, the bulk of the
pot landing on her palm, which must be
impervious to pain, because she doesn't yell
or cry out, simply takes it, absorbing the
blow, all of the liquid heat and force and
letting no harm come to your stupid little
head.

Already you can see the red marks forming
on her wrist and forearm, burns that will peel
then scar then darken and firm up into
reminders you'll see years later. After you've
gone to bed, you'll hear her walking up and
down the hall, going door to door asking your
neighbors for aloe, but no one has any or no
one has any that they are willing to part
with, so she'll settle for a small glob of
cold toothpaste daubed onto the spot, left
there thick and mint-green. You lie awake,
hearing her come back into the room, bracing
yourself for her wrath or fury or guilt trip,

but instead you get something else entirely. Tenderness. A softening in her eyes. It's the only thing worse than anger: advice.

> KUNG FU KID
> I'm sorry, Ma. I'm really sorry.

> MA
> (waving you off)
> I don't care about that. Just promise me something, okay?

> KUNG FU KID
> Okay.

> MA
> Don't grow up to be Kung Fu Guy.

> KUNG FU KID
> Okay, okay, I promise.
> (then)
> Wait, what?

> MA
> You heard me. Don't be Kung Fu Guy.

> KUNG FU KID
> Oh. Then what should I be?

> MA
> Be more.

Lying there in the silence, you try to imagine

what she could possibly mean. Kung Fu Guy is the pinnacle. How could anyone be more?

INT. CHINATOWN SRO

Most nights in the SRO you go to bed a little hungry. Which is made worse by having to wait until one or even two in the morning to take a shower, the better to avoid the long wait, people lined up all the way down the hallway and into the stairwell, holding their toothbrushes, towels slung over their shoulders, reading the paper, gossiping, staring at the walls. Nighttime is a battle against boredom and hunger and heat and humidity. By midnight, your stomach's making all kinds of noises, and it becomes a game to imagine that the various gurgly complaints coming from your abdomen are actually your internal organs' way of communicating very specific things to you ("How about a McDonald's Quarter Pounder" or "What if you cooked your shoe?" or "What if you cooked your shoe with some garlic and chili sauce?"). A damp washcloth thrown in the freezer and pulled out later can be a treat, if someone else doesn't get to it first.

Once in a long while, late-night fever takes hold of the building, spreads down one hallway then up and down the stairwells like wildfire. Frustration boils into indignation which condenses into something like, how funny is this shit? Because at some point,

this shit kinda is funny. Someone says to
hell with it and digs out from the back of
the icebox the flank steak they're supposed
to be saving, throws it into a pan, and
fries it up with onions and mushrooms,
slices bok choy and ginger and garlic,
sizzle and grease and the smell floating
down and up and all through the corridor. A
teenager turns on some music. Once that gets
going, doors start opening until they're all
open, the whole building buzzing until
sunrise, as if nothing matters because
nothing does matter because the idea was you
came here, your parents and their parents
and their parents, and you always seem to
have just arrived and yet never seem to have
actually arrived. You're here, supposedly, in
a new land full of opportunity, but somehow
have gotten trapped in a pretend version of
the old country.

INT. CHINATOWN SRO—EIGHTH FLOOR

You drift off for a while, only realizing you
were asleep at the exact moment you wake,
roused by the familiar and obnoxious sound of
idiots trash-talking one another in various
dialects. You open the door to find them all
hanging out, shouting, playing cards, seems
like every male in the building is there,
crowded around your door. The Generic Asian
Men, except up here they've got names:
    The usual suspects. Chen, Lin, Ling, Fong.

And, it goes without saying Huang, Hung, Chang, Li.

Lee, Lim, Wu, Wang.

But also Chu, Yang, Chiu, Tsai, Liao, Fu, Hsieh.

And even Tang, Mo, Dai, Yan, Zhang, Gong, Gu.

Not to mention Long, Jiang, Meng, Bai, Wei, Yu.

Pan, Peng, Ng, Lam, Yip, Sam.

You poke your head out and they pull you by the arms into the hallway.

I'm in my underwear, you say, but half of them are, too. By choice.

Someone slaps you on the back. Sup Willis.

Cousin Tsai, man, how you doing? You call him cousin because your moms are cool.

Someone starts talking smack.

Hey hey, everyone listen up.

What?

I'm gonna tell you something.

What?

I'm going to get the part.

You? You?

What? Why not me? I have good hair.

Yeah, but you're short.

We're the same height.

Bullshit.

I bench more than all of you.

You saying we're weak?

No one said that.

So you do think I'm weak.

I didn't say that. You said that.

Said what.

That you're weak.

Say it again.

I didn't say that. But I have no problem saying it to your face. You're weak.

Say it to my face.

I just did.

You're just jealous because my Wing Chun is the best.

No it's not. Anyway, it's not about Wing Chun anymore. They want flashy kicks.

No they don't. They don't even know what Wing Chun is. They want Taekwondo.

They want Chinese punching and Korean kicks.

They don't know what they want. They want cool Asian shit.

Finally, agreement all around. Cool Asian shit is what they want. If you could only figure out what that means.

You say, what makes any of you think it's going to be different this time?

What do you mean?

Maybe they make one of us Kung Fu Guy. Maybe a few good scenes. Maybe a poster, in the back, real small. And then what?

Silence. They all know you're right.

A beat.

Then Chiu says, man Willis, why you always gotta be such a downer? The other guys all agree and go back to playing cards.

INT. CHINATOWN SRO—EIGHTH FLOOR—YOUR
ROOM—NIGHT

The main thing about living on eight is that the shower pan in the bathroom on nine is cracked. It was cracked when you were a kid, crammed in this room with your parents, and it's still cracked now. They've repaired it a half-dozen times in the past few years but always on the cheap, caulking it with cheap stuff when what they really need to do is replace the whole damn thing. Otherwise, it will just keep cracking over and over again. As, everyone knows, water hates poor people. Given the opportunity, water will always find a way to make poor people miserable, typically at the worst time possible.

Which, for those living on the eighth floor, means that every time Old Fong (903) falls asleep in the shower, or Wang Tai Tai (908), or any one of the other Old Asian People up there on nine forgets to shut off the faucet (or can't shut it tight, on account of rheumatoid arthritis or carpal tunnel or general infirmity), after about five minutes, the whole pan floods, which means, for those of us down here on eight (and parts of seven on this side of the building), you're sleeping in half a foot of water for the next several nights. One time it went all the way down to six and soaked the little seat cushion that Baby Huang was sleeping on facedown, and Baby Huang sucked gray water through nylon for a couple minutes before her mom woke up to the dripping on her own head, found her little girl looking a strange color. The baby lived, but to this day whenever you see her running down the hall trying to keep up with the other kids, all you can hear is her sloshy wheeze.

She seems a little slow, although her dad, who is so nice everyone calls him Nice Guy Huang, is pretty slow himself (he's never even managed to become a Generic Asian Man, stuck in non-speaking), so who knows, maybe the whole almost drowning in her own crib didn't affect Baby Huang that much after all. Not like she was going to the Olympics anyway. Mostly she's growing up to be a pretty happy kid, living in this building, in Chinatown, it's fine. She doesn't know any better.

INT. CHINATOWN SRO—NIGHT

Old Fong fell asleep in the shower again. You know because the water stains on the ceiling are starting to darken and get puffy. In about ten minutes, it'll be raining inside your bedroom.

INT. CHINATOWN SRO—LITTLE LATER

It's raining inside your bedroom. You hope Old Fong is enjoying his nap.

INT. CHINATOWN SRO—HALLWAY—LATER

Shit. You were wrong. Old Fong didn't fall asleep in the shower. He died there.
    Someone knocked on the door, telling him his phone was ringing. Old Fong's son, Young

Fong, calls once a week, to check on his father. Old Fong usually sits on his bed all day, unwilling to move. He never misses that call. He'll nibble on a cracker, or maybe listen to the radio at an inaudibly low level. Maybe glance at the Taiwanese newspaper. But mostly, he just stares at his ancient rotary phone, waiting for it to ring.

The story, apparently, is that Old Fong waited all day, and Young Fong didn't call, because he had to work an extra shift and by the time he got home, Young Fong figured it was too late. So he called the next morning, right when Old Fong had stepped into the shower. Old Fong heard it and, excited to talk to his son, tried to get out, slipped and hit his head on the molded soap holder protruding from the shower wall.

Fatty Choy was apparently the one who found him. For once, Choy didn't have much to say. He was quiet for a long time. It took a shot of warm Christian Brothers and half a can of Coors Light to get him to stop crying. Then Fatty sat there stone-faced for another half-hour before explaining what happened.

Found him on the ground, Fatty says between slugs of beer. The water pooling. Must have hit the corner of the sink. Head getting soft like a fruit.

"He kept asking me," he says, "one eye shut. Asking what happened to his head."

INT. CHINATOWN SRO—LATE NIGHT

Young Fong's here, to collect his father's
things. Everyone's standing around now, trying
to figure out what to say at a moment like
this. Wang Tai Tai opens her mouth to speak,
her voice not much more than a warble.

                    WANG TAI TAI
          You were a good son.

                    YOUNG FONG
          Thank you, Wang Tai Tai.

                    WANG TAI TAI
          You shouldn't feel bad.

                    YOUNG FONG
          I don't. Well, I didn't. But now I kind
          of do.

Old Chan shushes Wang Tai Tai, scowls at her.
She scowls back. She's better at scowling than
Old Chan.
    You're exhausted, but there's no way you'll
be able to go back to bed. So you bum a
cigarette off of Skinny Lee on the fifth
floor, and come out here to smoke it.
    You keep thinking about Old Fong. Not that
he died alone. Not that he died naked, or wet,
or with soap on half his body. That he died
waiting for his son's phone call. That he
lived, absolutely sure that one person in the
world would always care, would always remember

to check in on him. And then in his last moment, he was unsure of whether that was still true.

Young Fong packs his father's things. A simple action, done carefully, turns into something more. He drags an old steamer trunk into the room to collect the belongings, carefully tucking each item into place. Smoothing out the threadbare clothes, as if his father might need them again. Treating the broken, the inexpensive, the humblest of possessions with dignity, just as Old Fong had taught him to do.

Standing there in the hall, you watch through the doorway, pretending you're not watching through the doorway. Has he forgotten you're back here, or does he just not care? The latter, you think. Young Fong isn't performing for twelve million people a week, or even twelve, by this point the rest of the SRO's inhabitants having mostly drifted away. When he's done, Young Fong inspects the room one last time, then turns toward his father's empty bed and lowers his head to say goodbye.

INT. GOLDEN PALACE—AFTER CLOSING

Back inside, the restaurant is closed. The tables are cleaned, the kitchen is dark.

It's karaoke time at the Golden Palace Chinese Restaurant.

After all the patrons have finished their smirky renditions of Marvin Gaye or Stevie

Wonder, tourists tipsy on one too many lychee margarita-tinis done wailing Whitney or Céline a half-step flat, after all of that it's the staff's turn at the microphone. And they don't waste it. Off-duty busboys warble *corridos* between long pulls from cans of Tecate, buried in their twang about a dozen different emotions you forgot you had. But even they're just the warm-up for the main event. At the appointed hour, right on time, he appears at the foot of the stage.

Old Asian Man is on the mic.

Everything goes silent while he adjusts his glasses, wipes his forehead, takes a sip of water.

"For my friend Fong," he says, and begins singing John Denver. If you didn't know it already, now you do: old dudes from rural Taiwan are comfortable with their karaoke and when they do karaoke for some reason they love no one like they love John Denver.

Maybe it's the dream of the open highway. The romantic myth of the West. A reminder that these funny little Orientals have actually been Americans longer than you have. Know something about this country that you haven't yet figured out. If you don't believe it, go down to your local karaoke bar on a busy night. Wait until the third hour, when the drunk frat boys and gastropub waitresses with headshots are all done with Backstreet Boys and Alicia Keys and locate the slightly older Asian businessman standing patiently in line for his turn, his face warmly rouged on Crown or Japanese lager, and when he steps up and starts slaying "Country Roads," try not to laugh, or wink knowingly or clap a little too hard, because by the time he gets to "West Virginia, mountain mama," you're going to be singing along, and by the time he's done, you might understand why a seventy-seven-year-old guy from a tiny island in the Taiwan Strait who's been in a foreign country for two-thirds of his life can nail a song, note perfect, about wanting to go home.

BLACK AND WHITE
PRODUCTION NOTES

MAKEUP

Taped eyelids
Heavy coloring, emphasizing skin tone

SET DESIGN

Curved eaves
Massive roofs
Pay attention to cornices!
Oriental flourishes and touches
Details are everything

INT. GOLDEN PALACE CHINESE RESTAURANT—NIGHT

Dead Asian Guy is still dead. The Impossible Crimes Unit is on the case.

                    GREEN
         Let's try to be sensitive here.

                    TURNER
         I'm always sensitive.

Green gives him a look. Then she freezes. She holds up a finger, silencing Turner.

                    GREEN
         Wait.
             (hears something)
         You hear that?
         Look—

Miles turns to see who Sarah is looking at: an OLD ASIAN MAN, maybe 70 (although, honestly, if you said anything between 48 and 88 we'd believe you—it's hard to tell with Asians. If black don't crack then yellow just kind of mellows).

    Old Asian Man has an upright bearing, and despite a softness in and around his midsection, in his posture and the precision of his movements there is the sense of an acquired discipline, something that suggests a deep awareness of his body and surroundings earned through a lifetime of focused training.

Green looks at Turner, who now looks less sure of himself.

                    TURNER
          Go ahead. You talk first.

                    GREEN
          Really? Why?

                    TURNER
          He might be scared of me. A lot of
          older Asians are pretty racist.
              (off her look)
          Sorry. It's true.

Green steps to Old Asian Man.

                    GREEN (CONT'D)
          Hello sir.
              (quick flash of badge)
          Have a second? We'd like to ask you a
          few questions.

Turner has a hand on his weapon. Green looks at Turner as in: come on dude. Really?
   Turner looks at Green like: what?
   Green looks at Turner like: the gun?
   Turner rolls his eyes like: fine.
   He reluctantly stands down. Clenches his jaw muscle. It looks awesome when he does this. People like the clenching, so Turner clenches a lot.

TURNER
The dead Chinese guy. Did you know him?

Old Asian Man doesn't answer, the physiognomy
of his exotic Eastern features, as
exacerbated by the repressive conditioning of
his Confucian worldview, turning his face
into an emotionless mask. Foreign, unknowable
even to the trained eye of these Western
detectives, the titular Black and White not
sure what to make of this strange little
yellow man, trying to discern what he's
feeling inside.

TURNER (CONT'D)
Hey. You. I'm talking to you.

Turner's playing the tough, so Green can
counter with tact. She softens, her body
language, her tone. The light shifts, and it's
tight on Green, her face center-frame, beauty
shot. Her hair shimmers.

GREEN
(sensitive, sincere)
What my partner's trying to say is, did
you have any relationship with the
deceased?

Turner stands down. He clenches again, to show
annoyance. Sexy, sexy annoyance.
Old Asian Man looks down at his feet.
Turner shifts his weight, nervous.

                    GREEN (CONT'D)
        Sir?

                       TURNER
                  (to Green)
        I don't think he understands you.

Turner turns toward Old Asian Man, stoops down
a little.

                    TURNER (CONT'D)
                  (little too loud)
        Do you understand her?

                       GREEN
        Sir? Do you understand?
                  (to Turner)
        We need a translator.

                       TURNER
        He knows something.

                       GREEN
        Even if he could understand us, I'm not
        sure he'll talk.

                       TURNER
        Maybe he'll be more talkative after a
        ride downtown.

Turner goes for his handcuffs.

Watching Old Asian
Man there with
nothing to do but
suffer silently.
To give Black and
White something
to react to.

You're so deep in the
background, you're
almost out of frame.
The script doesn't
give you anything
to say, your only
action to sweep the
floor. And watch your
father get talked
to like that. It's
his reaction that
breaks something
inside of you. Or
his nonreaction.
That this is who he
is, Old Asian Man.
Nothing more. His
acceptance of the
role. You have to do
something. You step
into focus.

Green turns to look at you. Turner draws his
weapon.

                    TURNER
Hands where we can see them.

                    GREEN
        (to Turner)
Will you stop it with the gun?

Turner lowers his firearm slowly. Green
approaches, gets close enough to your face
that you can smell her expensive perfume, see
how good her bone structure is.
   She looks into your eyes.

                    GREEN
And who are you?
        (slowly, a little loud)
Sir, please identify yourself.

              GENERIC ASIAN MAN
I'm no one. But I might be able to
help you.

Green and Turner look at each other.

                    GREEN
        (to you)
Excuse us for a minute.

They sidebar.

                    TURNER
Can we trust him?

                    GREEN
Not sure we have a choice. We need
someone to help us get around this
place.
    (then)
Chinatown is a different world.

                    TURNER
Sarah.

                    GREEN
What?

                    TURNER
You know I was an East Asian Studies
minor—

                    GREEN
At Yale. Yes I know, Miles.
Look, it's cool that you can order dim
sum. But with all due respect, a
semester of Cantonese isn't going to cut
it. This is a tight-knit community.
They'll close ranks, protect their own.
    (then)
If we want the real story, we need
someone on the inside.

Green turns to look at you. It's one of her
signature moves, a piercing, investigatory
gaze at the subject of her attention. This is
what makes her the best cop on the force. Her
ability to see right through to the heart of
things.

To make suspects wither, to give witnesses the courage to tell the truth. Also, her skin tone is so even. It's like she doesn't have pores at all.

                    GREEN
              (turns to you)
          You speak English well.

                    GENERIC ASIAN MAN
          Thank you.

                    TURNER
          Really well. It's almost like you don't have an accent.

Shit. Right. You forgot to do the accent.

                    TURNER
          So can you help us or not?

                    GENERIC ASIAN MAN
              (slight accent)
          You want me—to be policeman?

                    GREEN
          We want your help.
              (then)
          The victim's brother, his older brother, has gone missing.

This is your chance.
    You turn to Green and Turner. You say your line, remembering to do the accent.

GENERIC ASIAN MAN
Okay. I help you.

Oriental music plays as we

SMASH TO BLACK

. . . built with an architect, a set designer, and a construction superintendent from the Paramount lot. It featured rickshaw rides for tourists and numerous curio stalls that employed Chinese merchants in costume.

Bonnie Tsui

In the morning, you do the cop show.

In the afternoon, you do the cop show.

You get your envelope.

Ninety bucks for being Generic Asian Man.

You train. You stay in shape. You get ready for your next role.

Slowly, you climb the ladder:

Generic Asian Man Number Three.

Generic Asian Man Number Two.

You practice the words you will have to say.

"I did it for my family's honor, officer."

"I have disgraced my family, and now I must pay the price."

"Without face, I have nothing."

"Honor means everything in my culture. You . . . wouldn't understand."

You climb the ladder. Generic Asian Man Number One. You say the words. You train. You stay in shape. You do the cop show. You're close now. Close enough to imagine a different life.

INT. UNMARKED POLICE CAR

Monday morning. A new week. Black and White up front. You in back. Special Guest Star.

> TURNER
> Let's recap.

> GREEN
> You don't have to say that.

TURNER

Don't have to say what?

GREEN

"Let's recap."

TURNER

Recapping is important. People like to
be sure of where they are.

GREEN

I'm not saying recapping isn't
important. I'm saying you don't have to
say "let's recap."

TURNER

What should I say?

GREEN

Don't say anything.

TURNER

(to you)
Can you believe this?

No, you think. You can't believe it. How much
fun they're having. How little they care. An
Asian guy is dead, and these two are flirting.
It's easy to squander your lines when you know
there will always be more tomorrow. And the
next day, and the day after that.

GREEN

Fine. To recap:
Dead Asian Guy is dead.

> TURNER

Could be gang-related.

> SPECIAL GUEST STAR
> (that's you!)

No. He would never doing a crime.

> GREEN

Some kind of honor killing then.

> TURNER

Those are common in Chinatown.

> SPECIAL GUEST STAR

They are not. None of this sound like him. Not possible.

> TURNER

Why? Because you say so?

> SPECIAL GUEST STAR

If you no need my help, I go back to restaurant.

> TURNER

Yeah, why don't you do that.
While you're back there, get me a lunch special. Number five, beef broccoli.

> GREEN

Miles! What the hell.
> (to you)

I'm sorry about that.

Turner looks chastened. Maybe a little embarrassed. It feels good to have WHITE on your side.

                    TURNER
          (to you)
          I don't know why I said that, man.
          That's not really who I am.

You pause to consider this. Green snaps you out of it.

                    GREEN
          Patrol's sweeping the area for
          eyewitnesses.

                    TURNER
          All these eyes.
          Someone saw something.

                    GREEN
          (to you)
          Did he have any enemies? Someone he had
          trouble with?

                    SPECIAL GUEST STAR
          No way.

Green gives Turner a meaningful look.

                    TURNER
          Are you trying to give me a meaningful
          look?

                    GREEN
This is my thing. My thing is this
look.

                    TURNER
You should consider getting another
thing.

                    GREEN
Look who's talking.

                    TURNER
What's that supposed to mean?

                    GREEN
      (sultry)
I'm Miles Turner. My jaw is so strong
and sexy.

            SPECIAL GUEST STAR
Should we focus here? Dead guy still
dead. And now Older Brother missing.

Uh oh. They both turn to look at you.

                    TURNER
Older Brother? You knew him?

            SPECIAL GUEST STAR
Everyone knew him. Everyone look up to
Older Brother. He was number one. No
one could ever beat him.

Green looks at Turner. Turner looks at Green.

They both look at you. You look at them. Green looks back at Turner. Turner looks back at you.

> SPECIAL GUEST STAR
> What?

> TURNER
> WHAT WHAT?

> SPECIAL GUEST STAR
> Why you guys keep giving each other looks?

> GREEN
> You said no one could ever beat Older Brother.

> SPECIAL GUEST STAR
> Yeah. So?

> TURNER
> Sounds like possible motive to me.

> SPECIAL GUEST STAR
> What motive?

> GREEN
> If someone were to knock him off—

> TURNER
> There's suddenly an opening. An opportunity.

                    SPECIAL GUEST STAR
           For who?

                         GREEN
           Every other Asian man in Chinatown.

                    ATTRACTIVE OFFICER
                (approaches)
           Haven't gotten an address yet.

                         GREEN
           Well what did you get?

                    ATTRACTIVE OFFICER
                (hands her slip of paper)
           Last known contact was with Ming-Chen
           Wu.

Green looks at the name, then looks at you.

                         GREEN
           Wu. Any relation?

                    SPECIAL GUEST STAR
           We're not all related.

                        TURNER
           Don't lie to us. Do you know him?

                    SPECIAL GUEST STAR
           Okay, yes. In this case, I happen
           to know him. But my point still
           stands.

                        TURNER
            Shut up and take us to him.

And then there's the GONG SOUND again. You
look around but can't tell where it's coming
from.

INT. GOLDEN PALACE—FRONT OF HOUSE

You enter the restaurant, a step behind Black
and White, your eyes still adjusting to the
low light. Soft music plays. Attractive extras
nibble on beef chow fun. You look around,
don't see anyone you know. Green and Turner
look to you. You motion toward the kitchen.

                  SPECIAL GUEST STAR
            In the back.

INT. GOLDEN PALACE—KITCHEN

As you push through the swinging door, a wave
of grease hits first, followed by curse words
in seven different dialects. The staff all
turn and look. Your friends and neighbors,
rivals and fellow kung fu students, dressed as
prep cooks and dishwashers, looking at you
with a mixture of envy and pride. This is the
moment you've dreamt of. Coming back here, not
as one of them, but as a star. Okay not a
star yet. But someone on the rise. An Asian
Man who gets to talk.

Old Asian Man is in the corner. You go to him quickly, to have a word in private before Green and Turner catch up.

"Ba," you say, under your breath. He's manning the deep fryer, in a stained undershirt, hair pulled back and tucked under the edges of a white paper hat. As if this were the most natural thing in the world. As if this were all he'd ever done for half a century. As if he hadn't been a dragon, once, not that long ago, hadn't fought epic battles on the streets of Chinatown, and above its rooftops. None of that matters now. None of that counts toward the final tally. Now he's this: a leading man trapped in the body of an extra. He looks tired. He is tired. He spent decades in this place, in the interior of Chinatown, taking the work he could get. Gangster, cook, inscrutable, mystical, nonsensical Oriental.

Now trapped in the back of the house, speaking lines that need subtitles. Thousands of hours of work at something and then in a moment, the work gone. Kung fu master to fry cook, the easiest transition in the world. Change wardrobe, hair, a career forgotten. A lifetime repurposed. A kind of amnesia that he has internalized, a fog of amnesia that hangs over this whole place.

Keng-chhat u bun-te, you say, under your breath, probably mangling it, but he knows what you mean, can decipher your clumsy pronunciation. *The police have questions*. You say it not in Mandarin, but Taiwanese. The family language, the inside language. A secret code.

He acknowledges this with the smallest shift in his eyes.

The kitchen staff run interference, getting in the way of Black and White, giving you just a few extra moments with your dad. He says something you don't quite follow. You hear it, you catch most of the individual words, and yet somehow—you don't understand. This gap, always there. Somehow unbridgeable, whether it's across a wide Pacific gulf of language and culture, or just a simple sentence, father to son, always distance. The texture of everyday actions, simple movements and gestures, is harder than it looks. The great shame of your life that you can't speak his language, not really, not fluently.

"Have you eaten yet, Dad?"

"Yes yes. Are you okay, Willis?"

"Why?"

He flits his eyes toward Green and Turner.

"I'm working with them now. This could be good."

"Happy for you," he says. He looks skeptical.
Worried.

Turner and Green, pushing past all the Chinamen, finally reach you. They look suspicious.

GREEN
What were you saying to him?

SPECIAL GUEST STAR
Nothing. I am saying nothing.

TURNER
Didn't look like nothing.

SPECIAL GUEST STAR
Okay, okay. I was asking old man if
knowing something.

Old Asian Man looks at you, a look of
disappointment flickering across his features
with each accented word. You playing this
part, talking like a foreigner. The son who
was born here, raised here, a stranger to his
own dad for what. For this. So he could be
part of this, part of the American show, black
and white, no part for yellow. The son who got
As in every subject, including English, now
making a living as Generic Asian Man.
    "I wanted better for you," he says.
    "Dad," you start, but you don't know what
to say.
    "Don't say anything? There is nothing left
to say."
    "Mom said something earlier. Are you—Ba,
are you okay?"
    He looks down. He's not okay.
    Turner breaks the silence.

TURNER
What's going on here? The real story.

What does he mean? Your dad—his actual

struggles. It's all you have left. Can you
trust him not to take it away from you? There
appears to be more to Turner and Green than
you once thought. But it's too risky. You've
worked too hard to show them something they
might not understand. You need to keep it
together. You can't get fired now. You make
your face into a mask—dead in the eyes. Not a
person. Not a real one anyway. A type.
Generic. It's a form of protection. Keep
yourself inside this costume, this role. You
lay it on a little thicker with the accent,
break up your grammar a bit more.

> SPECIAL GUEST STAR
> I was just explain to him Older Brother
> is missing. To answer all of your
> questioning so can be helpful to
> detectives in the case.

Turner sees that you're back on script, gets
back into character himself.

> TURNER
> Is he going to help?

> SPECIAL GUEST STAR
> He say he will help as much as he can.
>   (then)
> You know, he used to be someone. A
> teacher. Kung fu.

Turner appraises Old Asian Man.

                    TURNER
So this is him, huh? The master?

                SPECIAL GUEST STAR
Yes. He was my teacher. Taught everyone
in Chinatown. When he was young man, he
was incredible. He could show you some
things.

                    TURNER
Show me some things?
    (laughs)
Okay.

                SPECIAL GUEST STAR
You have muscles, yes, but here,
inside, you are soft. I can see it. You
move slow, like a turtle.

                    TURNER
I'll show you how I move, you little—

Green pulls Turner aside, out of earshot. Or
so they think.

                    GREEN
Take it easy.

                    TURNER
Why? He started all of this.

                    GREEN
Yeah, maybe he did. But we need him, if
we're going to get anywhere in

> Chinatown. Just—be nice to the Asian
> Guy, okay?

There we go. The two words: Asian Guy. Even
now, as Special Guest Star, even here, in your
own neighborhood. Two words that define you,
flatten you, trap you and keep you here. Who
you are. All you are. Your most salient
feature, overshadowing any other feature about
you, making irrelevant any other characteristic.
Both necessary and sufficient for a complete
definition of your identity: Asian. Guy.

> SPECIAL GUEST STAR
> You know, I can hear everything you're
> saying. That's what I am, huh? Asian
> Guy.

Green looks sheepish.

> GREEN
> I didn't mean—

> SPECIAL GUEST STAR
> Sure you didn't.

> TURNER
> There are worse things to be called.

> SPECIAL GUEST STAR
> Yeah?

> TURNER
> Yeah.

(then)
Anyway, weren't you the one who took
the role? You want to know the truth?
You did this to yourself.

SPECIAL GUEST STAR
I'm choosing this?

TURNER
No. But you're going along with it.
Look where we are. Look what you
made yourself into. Working your
way up the system doesn't mean
you beat the system. It
strengthens it. It's what the
system depends on.

SPECIAL GUEST STAR
You're part of the system. Your face is
on the poster. Your name is in the
title.

TURNER
I am? It says Miles Turner? No, it
doesn't.
It says: black.
(then)
I'm not a person. I'm a category.
Giving me the lead doesn't make me any
more of a person. If anything, less. It
locks me in. Do you know where I
started? Do you know what it took? You
can't come in here, five minutes ago,
talking about how hard you have it. If

you don't like it here, go back to
China.

With both hands, you push Turner in the chest.
He stumbles back, but catches himself. Wow.
His pecs are like concrete. Round, smooth,
pec-shaped slabs of concrete.

Turner gets up in your face. He's got four
inches and forty pounds on you, all of it
muscle.

But your kung fu is solid, and getting
better every day, and for a second, you
wonder, what would Older Brother do? You
wonder: could you take him?

He clenches his jaw, puts up his fists, like
he wants to box. You get into a solid fighting
stance. Your left foot tingles, ready for
action. It's in the eyes, you remember your
training. And for a half-second, you see in
Turner's eyes the smallest flicker of doubt.

GREEN
All right break it up.

SPECIAL GUEST STAR
That's right. Listen to your partner,
Miles.

TURNER
You really like that, don't you? When
Green sticks up for you. Feels good to
have WHITE on your side, don't it? Have
her approval.

SPECIAL GUEST STAR
You calling me a model minority?

TURNER
You said it, I didn't. Don't you see?
This is how it works. We're fighting
with each other. I don't want to be
doing this any more than you do. And
Green gets to be the bigger person. Why
do you care what she thinks anyway? You
heard what you are to her: Asian Guy.

GREEN
Feel better? More manly? Hope you got
it all out of your system so we can
get back to work.

Green turns to Old Asian Man, watching this.
Unsure of how to deal with him. He's not a
threat, not a rival, not a subordinate or
superior. Definitely not a potential love
interest, no no, come on, he's an Old Asian
Man—now you know, that's how she thinks of
him. And you. And all of you. She stoops down
a couple of inches, talks to him.

GREEN (CONT'D)
Hello sir. Thank you for your help.

Talks to him a little louder than normal, more
than a little, half-shouting almost, as if
he's hard of hearing, while also doing the
thing. You know the thing that people do
sometimes with Old Asian People. The sort of

half-assed sign language except it's not sign
language at all, just a made-up pantomime, as
if Old Asians won't otherwise be able to
understand anything you're saying. As if it
takes all of this effort just to get through
to this other consciousness. As if he's an
alien.

                    TURNER
            (to Old Asian Man)
        Older Brother. When did you last see
        him?

Old Asian Man looks at you. As if to ask you:
Is this what you want? For me to answer? You
nod. He hesitates briefly, then answers.

                OLD ASIAN MAN
        Long time. Been a long time.

                    GREEN
        Weeks?

                OLD ASIAN MAN
        Longer. Six month, maybe.
            (then)
        We have argument.

                    TURNER
        About what?

                OLD ASIAN MAN
        What else. Money.

> GREEN
As in, he wanted to borrow money?

> OLD ASIAN MAN
> (shaking his head)
Not borrow. Give. He want to give me
money. But I don't want it.

Green and Turner look at each other. Then at
you.

> GREEN
Older Brother shows up, trying to give
away money.

> TURNER
Laundering?

> GREEN
Possibly. In any case, sounds like he
had a sudden windfall.

> TURNER
We follow the money—

> GREEN
We find our guy.

They're looking at each other now, their faces
having somehow gotten pretty close in the
course of this last exchange. Are they going to
kiss? That would be weird. But it seems like
they're going to kiss. They should just kiss.
But then again, they shouldn't, because if they

ever did, that would be that, no one would care
anymore. The whole point is that they never do.
They get their faces all close and they smolder
and they gaze but they never kiss. Turner
finally breaks eye contact and looks at you.

                    TURNER
          (to you)
          So where is it? Where's the money in
          Chinatown?

                    GREEN
          This is important. If you know
          something, you have to tell us.

Are you doing the right thing? Something about
this feels wrong.
     But this is Black and White. They let you
have a part. You can't stop now.
     You look at your dad. He shifts his eyes
away, and you know in that moment that he is
disappointed. But he won't ever say it. You'll
never talk about it again. He's gone, slipped
back into Old Asian Man. He's not going to make
the choice for you. It's your role to play.

                    SPECIAL GUEST STAR
          Okay.

                    TURNER
          Okay?

                    SPECIAL GUEST STAR
          I take you there. I will take you
          inside Chinatown.

INT. CHINATOWN GAMBLING DEN

Fatty Choy is working the door. You slap
hands, do a one-arm guy hug.
    "Congrats, man," he says under his breath.
Turner gives him the once-over, gets up in his
personal space.

                    TURNER
            (gruff)
        We need to see your boss.

Fatty Choy's face transforms. One moment he's
your boy from the SRO, the next moment he's
disappeared, turned into a Lowlife Oriental.

                    LOWLIFE ORIENTAL
        Sorry. Private club. No outsider
        allowed in here.

                    TURNER
        I got a private club for you. It's
        downtown at the precinct. I'll book a
        room and give you a lift—

                    LOWLIFE ORIENTAL
        This is a place of business—

                    GREEN
        Wrong. This is an illegal gambling
        operation.

                    LOWLIFE ORIENTAL
        I don't know anything about no

gambling. I'm just security guard. You can't arrest me for me just doing my job.

                    TURNER
How about I arrest you for an aggravated assault last week? As well as public intoxication and a couple counts of resisting arrest? How's that sound, Choy? Yeah, we know who you are.

Turner looks smug as Fatty Choy steps aside. As you brush past, he mumbles something under his breath.

"Willis," he says.

"Yeah?"

"Hope you know what you're doing."

"Me too."

You make your way through the room hazy with cigarette smoke, the light click-clack of poker chips being stacked, shuffled, tossed around. Sultry Asian Women in high-slit dresses serve beers and whiskeys to Sleazy Asian Guys in white T-shirts and slacks. Everyone, men and women, young and old, looking sketchy, looking like they'll cut you for cheating or cut you for winning or just cut you if you look at them wrong. Or at least that's what they look like to an outsider. But you know these fools, grew up with most of them, playing Nintendo or sneaking sips of wine cooler from the fridge in the back of the grocery store on Ninth. Average GPA in this room is probably north of three point seven, and now look at them, pretending to be tough, doing a good job at it, as they do. They're all A students, striving immigrants, still hoping for their shot.

Above it all is the owner of this place, watching the tables from his second-floor office, one eye on the patrons, the other one on his employees.

Turner looks at Green, motions toward the stairs. Green plays it cool, sliding her hand just slightly toward the piece in her waistband as you climb the steps. Turner motions for you to enter first, the two of them falling in behind you.

INT. GAMBLING DEN—BOSS'S OFFICE—CONTINUOUS

As you reach the top of the stairs, the door opens. The Bad Guy of the Week steps out. It's Young Fong. His eyes still red and puffy, his dad not gone even three days and already here's Fong, back to work.

"Hey," you whisper, trying to think of the right thing to say. A kind word. But he plays it straight. Professional. At the moment he's not Fong. He is Chinatown Mini Boss. Medium fish in a small pond. The guy before the guy. Intermediate obstacle. An act two villain who gets you into act three. It's a good gig, even if Fong is starting to get typecast. Something about how gentle he is, they love to play off of that, love how his mild features, his

slender build and slightly pasty complexion,
make him the opposite of Turner, the opposite
of masculine, make this Asian phenotype
slightly and inherently creepy to the Western
eye.

                    MINI BOSS
          Detectives.
               (affected, enunciated)
          To what do I owe the pressure?

Turner straight-arms his way into the office.

                    TURNER
          Cut the shit. This isn't a social call.

                    MINI BOSS
          Oh. That's too bad. Chinatown has much
          to offer for the adventurous traveler.
               (to Turner)
          Those who want to sample its exotic
          flavors.

Fong looks down into the casino at the dozens
of Sultry Asian Women, as if to say, go ahead,
choose one. Turner coughs, uncomfortable,
adjusts himself. Fong gets up and pours
himself two generous fingers of expensive
Scotch.

                    MINI BOSS
          I'm sure we can find something to your
          liking.
               (looks at Green)

Whatever your type may be. We will
accommodate you.

Fong presses a button on the underside of
his desk, and a moment later a woman steps
into the office. Not just a woman. You
don't—you don't know what to. Uh. Say. Or
do. With your arms. Or face. You're frozen,
a schoolboy with a crush. You're an idiot.
Wow.
    She looks at you, and you look at her, and
she looks at you and you can't figure out why
she's looking at you, until you realize you're
staring at her. What—is she? You can't figure
it out.
    "Do I know you?" you whisper, but either
she doesn't hear or she ignores the question.

                    TURNER
        Enough bullshit. We're looking for
        someone.

                    MINI BOSS
        You have a warrant? Probable cause?

                    GREEN
        We have him.

She points to you. A beat. Silence. Everyone's
looking at you.

                    MINI BOSS
        Oh yeah? And who the hell is he?

                    GREEN
     He's working with us. Impossible Crimes
     Unit.

Turner looks at Green like, what? She looks at
you. You try really hard not to blush, but
your legs get weak and the skin on the back
of your neck gets tingly.

                    GREEN
          (to you)
     It's you, man. Your move.

You clear your throat, trying to sound like
you know what you're doing.

               SPECIAL GUEST STAR
     Older Brother is missing.

Your voice cracks a little. Turner giggles.

                  MINI BOSS
     I heard.

                    GREEN
     We learned that he had a fight with his
     father. He'd recently come into some
     money. Sounds like he was looking for a
     safe place to park it.

                  MINI BOSS
     And you think I had something to do
     with it?

                    TURNER
          (nods toward the casino)
     Seems like a pretty good option.

                    MINI BOSS
     Yeah. You're right. It does. Except
     if you knew anything about Older
     Brother, you'd know how stupid that
     is.
          (looks at you)
     Why didn't you tell them how stupid
     that is?

You do your best poker face, but you are bad
at poker. Green reads it on your face.

                    GREEN
     What does he mean?

                SPECIAL GUEST STAR
     Older Brother didn't care about money.
     At all.

                    MINI BOSS
     Anyone who knows him would understand
     that. He had a plan, but it had nothing
     to do with money.

Turner's ears perk up.

                    TURNER
     What kind of plan? You better talk
     or—

                    MINI BOSS
          Or what? Why should I tell you
          anything?

                    GREEN
          There are enough federal and state
          crimes being committed in this building
          to put you away for a very long time.
            (then)
          Unless, of course, you know something
          that could help us. Something that
          might make us inclined to go easy.

                    MINI BOSS
          I want immunity.

                    TURNER
          No can do. Not with what we have on
          you.

                    MINI BOSS
          I'm not negotiating.

                    TURNER
          Neither am I.

Turner clenches his jaw. You're not sure if
you want to punch his face or caress it.

                    GREEN
          We'll put in a good word with the DA's
          office. Get you the best deal they can
          manage.

                    TURNER
You might be able to get out to see
your children graduate from college.

                    MINI BOSS
Deal, huh? I'm a businessman,
detectives, and I know about deals.
That is a shit deal.

Fong gives a signal. From downstairs, the
sound of a bottle breaking against the craps
table. Someone lifts the roulette wheel off
its base and flings it across the room like a
solid oak Frisbee. It smashes into the bar,
spilling tequila and Corona and red wine
everywhere. Tables flipping, chips flying,
kung fu breaking out all over the place. Shots
fired, people diving for cover. Turner and
Green draw their weapons and run low toward
the window, trying to survey the situation. In
the chaos, Fong ducks out a secret exit,
leaving behind his mysterious beauty.

  "Uh," you say. Real smooth, dumbass. A
natural action hero.

  "Get low," she says, but it's not in the
script and you just stand there, frozen,
unsure of what you're supposed to do. She
dives, knocking you to the ground just as
glass explodes behind you in a spray of
bullets, the two of you tumbling to the
ground, faces close. It takes you a second to
register the fact that she saved your life.

  "I'm Karen," she says. Also not in the
script.

"Will," you say. "Willis Wu."

"Nice to meet you, Willis Wu."

A henchman appears in the doorway. It's Fatty Choy. You notice him a beat before anyone else and, in one continuous motion, kick up to your feet, execute a front handspring covering three-quarters of the distance, coming in not straight-on but at a right angle from your opponent's nondominant side, kick the gun out of his hand and watch it slide across the floor and stop right at Turner's feet. He turns around, still processing what just happened. You catch your breath. Whoa. You moved fast—faster than anyone in the room. That was some Older Brother–caliber fighting right there. You didn't even know you were capable. Even Sifu might have been impressed.

You pin Fatty to the ground, putting a knee in his back, iron grip on his wrists. Almost like you're a real cop.

"Ow," he groans, quietly. "Dude, give me a break."

Sorry, you say, easing off a little.

"It's cool, Willis. That was some hero shit right there. When did you get so good at kung fu?"

"I don't know," you say. "I guess I've been practicing."

"No shit," he says. "I can tell."

                    SPECIAL GUEST STAR
          Everyone okay?

Green picks herself up, brushes glass off.

                    GREEN
          Nice work.

Turner holsters his weapon, looks rattled.

                    TURNER
              (to you)
          That wasn't proper procedure.

                    GREEN
          Well he saved your ass, Miles.

                    TURNER
          Shit. Where'd Fong go?

Green finds the hidden door, slides it open
and closed.

                    GREEN
          Check it out. He got away.

Turner cuffs Fatty, roughs him up a bit,
slamming him down into a chair.

                    TURNER
          Talk. Your boss—does he know anything
          about Older Brother? Were they working
          together?

You talk in Fake Chinese to Fatty Choy, and he
pretends to answer in some gibberish he's
making up as he goes along. Then in real

Cantonese he says he's not telling you shit.
You turn to Green and Turner.

                SPECIAL GUEST STAR
     He says he doesn't know anything.

                WOMAN (O.S.)
     He's lying.

You turn toward the woman, surprised.

                GREEN
     Wu, this is Detective Karen Lee.
     Although looks like you two have
     already met.

You turn to look at her, trying not to faint.
Her cheekbones. Her earlobes. Her hair! Her
hair should be on a commercial.
  Karen Lee shakes your hand with an iron
grip, flashes a smile, and that's when you
realize where you've seen her before: she's
the woman from the poster. Floating behind
Black and White.

                SPECIAL GUEST STAR
     Thanks.

                LEE
     For what?

                SPECIAL GUEST STAR
     Uh, for saving my life?

                         LEE
        I know. I just wanted to hear you say
        it. Pretty good footwork back there,
        Will. We might be able to use a guy
        like you in undercover vice.

                   SPECIAL GUEST STAR
        You mean, like, a full-time role? Like—

                         LEE
        Kung Fu Guy? Maybe. Anything is
        possible.

She looks at her hand, which you're still
holding. You let it go. She smiles and leans
in. She smells so good.
   She whispers to you: Let me do the talking.
You nod, unsure why you're going along with
her, oh yeah, you are probably in love with
her already, that's why. She turns back to
Green.

                       LEE
        He knows something. But he'll never
        snitch.

                      TURNER
           (nods, clenches)
        Honor is very important to these
        people.

                       LEE
        Sure. Also, they'll kill his family.

                    GREEN
          (to Lee)
     You learn anything?

                    LEE
     You mean before you crashed my
     investigation and let the perp get
     away? Did I learn anything before all
     that shit happened?

                    GREEN
     I'm sorry it went down like that,
     Karen. But we'll get him.

                    TURNER
     Fong's probably halfway to Hong Kong by
     now. The money got away.

Lee holds up an Hermès bag.

                    LEE
     Nope. Here's the money.

Turner takes it, opens it, turns it over.

                    TURNER
     Empty.

                    LEE
     Not in the bag. The money is the bag.

                    GREEN
          (getting it)
     Counterfeit?

                    LEE
Fong was running fake luxury goods.
Chinatown's number one export.

                   GREEN
So what's our next move?

                    LEE
     (turns to you)
I bet you know where they make those
bags.

            SPECIAL GUEST STAR
     I do?

                    LEE
You do.

And then you understand. It's the bridge
into the next scene, how Black and White
works, the plot humming along from clue to
clue. You're along for the ride, part of the
story now. Just follow along, and she'll
keep you safe.

            SPECIAL GUEST STAR
     Right. I do.

                    LEE
Well, what are we waiting for? Let's
go.

Karen looks at you as if to say, you and
me, we're in this together. The way she

looks at you makes you melt a little bit
and then you realize your back is wet, and
you wonder if maybe you are actually
melting? You touch your shirt, which is
soaked with sweat from the fight, except
it's only on your right side, and you look
at your hand and see it's covered in blood,
just like the floor under you. A lot of
blood. Your blood. Which is when your legs
give out, and then you fall down.

>   GREEN
>   No!
>   (to a patrolman)
>   Get a medic here—this, uh, Asian Man
>   has been shot.

Turner takes a knee, crouching low to talk to
you.

>   TURNER
>   You helped our investigation.

>   SPECIAL GUEST STAR
>   Now you nice to me?

>   GREEN
>   I won't forget this. We won't forget
>   it. You have brought honor on your
>   family.

>   SPECIAL GUEST STAR
>   Wait, what?

                    TURNER
          You're dying, man.

                    SPECIAL GUEST STAR
          What? Already? Are you sure?

                    TURNER
          I'm sure.

                    SPECIAL GUEST STAR
          I don't understand. How can I be dying?
          I just made it.
               (to Karen)
          I just met you.

Detective Lee looks resigned, but unsurprised.

                    LEE
               I know, Will. I know. I wish it
               didn't have to be like this, but you
               know how it is. You're an Asian Man.
               Your story was great, while it
               lasted, but now it's done. I hope
               our paths cross again.
               Maybe somewhere else.

And you think: no. It won't be somewhere else.
It will be here, again, in Chinatown, next
year, same place. To be yellow in America. A
special guest star, forever the guest.

FADE TO BLACK

Behind many masks and many characters, each performer tends to wear
a single look, a naked unsocialized look, a look of concentration, a look of one who is privately engaged in a difficult, treacherous task.

Erving Goffman

Ever since you were a boy, you've dreamt of being Kung Fu Guy.

You are not Kung Fu Guy.

You were close there for a moment. But then you died.

DEATH

When you die, it sucks.

DEATH, PART II

The first thing that happens is you can't work
for forty-five days.

144 · CHARLES YU

By the coffee and donuts you run into a familiar face.

"Hey," you say. "Attractive Officer."

"Very Special Guest Star," she says. "Here we are."

"Surprised to see you here," you say. "Why would you be surprised?"

"It's *Black and White*," you say. "Thought you'd have a bigger part."

"Asian Men aren't the only invisible people around here, Willis. Look around."

You see what she means. A bunch of Asian dudes and Black women, nibbling on bear claws, stirring powdered creamer into paper cups.

"We should do our own thing, someday," she says. "*Black and Yellow*."

"You'll be, what? Ex-CIA?"

"Slash supermodel. Slash mother of four," she says. "Their dad takes care of the kids."

"And I'll be?"

"Whatever you want, man," she says. "A guy can dream," you say.

"Cheers to that." You touch your small coffee cups to each other's, a toast to something you both know will never happen.

DEATH, PART III

Why forty-five days? It's the minimum length necessary, just long enough for everyone to forget you existed.

Because even though you all look alike, it's still weird if you get murdered on Tuesday and by Thursday you're showing up in the background of a street scene or as a busboy.

Who knows how they calculate these things but someone did and figured out the optimal amount of time. Optimal for them, of course, not for you. Not for anyone who needs to make a living as a Delivery Guy, or a Busboy, or an Inscrutable Background Oriental. Not optimal at all. It feels like an eternity and no matter how much you might need the cash, whatever your sob story, sick baby, hungry kid, Mom needs her medicine, casting won't even touch you for the mandatory cooling-off period. Doesn't matter to them. When you're dead, you are nobody.

Some people think it isn't the worst thing in the world to die. Because if you never die—if you play the same role too long—you start to get confused. Forget who you really are.

Your mother used to die all the time. You always knew when it had happened, because on those days she'd pick you up from school and she'd have taken the pins out of her hair so it fell down to her shoulders and you always thought she looked so glamorous, with her hair like that, with the makeup from work still on. You'd go back to the SRO together and while you washed your face and neck and hands and changed into your sleep clothes she would make you a bowl of fried rice with an egg and a few pickles. Some of the happiest times of your life were when your mother was dead, because you knew it meant she would be home for six weeks, you would have her all to yourself in the afternoons. You would play with a toy or watch television and she would sit next to you, practicing her English while biding her time between lives, always preparing for her next role, however small, for a day, to be someone, if only for a short while.

When she was dead, she got to be your mother.

INT. AMERICAN MOVIES—1950S AND '60S

She'd once dreamed of being more. When she
first started out, as Young Asian Woman. She
imagined a life for herself, full of
romance, glamour. One of the few American
stories that had made its way to the silver
screen of Taipei in the '50s, an afternoon
at the cinema with her father and nine
sisters and brothers, sharing one Coke. Being
the eighth of ten, she might get one good
sip before it got taken back by siblings
further up the chain, but that one sip was
enough to savor, sitting up on her heels to
get a better view, holding her father's
hand, and watching the perfect faces, Grace
Kelly, Kim Novak, Natalie Wood, their
luminous whiteness shimmering in the cool,
darkened theater.

INT. THE MOVIE VERSION OF HER LIFE—NIGHT

She's in a wine red cheongsam, Mandarin
collar, short sleeves. Gold piping from neck
to bottom. Slits rising up each leg. Nat King
Cole on the jukebox, smoke rising from the
tips of cigarettes held by men sitting in twos
and threes, all heads turning as she descends
the stairs.
And now her costar makes his entrance, Old
Asian Man, but like her, he's young, dashing.
He sees her and is overcome by her beauty.

                    DASHING ASIAN MAN
          I've been looking for you.

                   PRETTY ASIAN HOSTESS
          That so? And now that you've found me,
          what do you have to say for yourself?

He opens his mouth, but the words won't come out.
   She waits in anticipation for him, but
there's no line for him, nothing he can say.
No stage direction, or action lines, or
parentheticals telling them what they're
thinking. He looks back at the door, and at
her, trying to remember, but it's already
slipping away. The outside, the world beyond.
A life they could have together, if only they
could figure a way out. Could rent a home or
even, dream of dreams, own one. Find a job,
new costumes, have names other than Asian
Woman, Asian Man.
   Instead, they remain here. In the smoky
room, she in her dress, he in his suit. As we
pull back, we see that this is a golden
palace, or it was, once. When the colors were
brighter, the music swingier. Now it's the
Golden Palace Chinese Restaurant.

INT. GOLDEN PALACE CHINESE RESTAURANT—NIGHT

No less radiant in her cheongsam, she doesn't
descend the stairs. Instead, she stands,
dutifully, at the hostess station, greeting
patrons as they enter.

He still wears his suit, but the tie is gone, the top button now open to reveal an undershirt damp with perspiration, his black slacks now worn thin in the knees from bending over in the walk-in freezer, from loading fifty-pound sacks of rice, from clearing tables of plates with steamed fish, braised pork, hot and sour soup.

After close, he lingers, waiting to see if she'll have some tea with him.

> ASIAN MAN/WAITER
> Do you have a name?

> PRETTY ASIAN HOSTESS
> Not really. No.

> ASIAN MAN/WAITER
> Why don't you give yourself one?

> PRETTY ASIAN HOSTESS
> You can do that?

> ASIAN MAN/WAITER
> Why not? It can just be for us. Didn't you have a name, that you liked? From the movies?

She thinks for a moment, then decides.

> PRETTY ASIAN HOSTESS
> Dorothy. I'll call myself Dorothy. And you? What should I call you?

ASIAN MAN/WAITER
You can call me Wu. Ming-Chen Wu.

They talk easily, sharing a cigarette, pot
after pot of oolong or, her favorite,
chrysanthemum, trading backstories.
    She'd come from a hard background in the old
country, and he smiles in recognition, me too,
me too, both of them laughing—Striving
Immigrant was the only kind of work they could
get. Still, they were appreciative. This was a
plot that had a shape to it, something
understandable. Tiny, anonymous parts for each
of them, an undercurrent of social or
political relevance. Hard to see the big
picture from their vantage point, but they
knew that behind them was a historical
backdrop, that they were part of a prestigious
project, with the sweep and scope of a grand
American narrative. So they do what it takes,
make the best of a small role, just to get in.

INT. DOROTHY'S BACKSTORY—HOSPITAL—DAY

She as a nurse's assistant, a yellow girl
living in Alabama in 1969. Scale then was a
dollar seventy-five an hour, and then a
twenty-five-cent raise, making two bucks even,
helping to give sponge baths to the older
patients, fending off looks and wandering
hands. Hey come here, hey you China doll, with
the porcelain skin and almond eyes, let me get
a look at those slim thighs, and then when the

advances were politely yet firmly rebuffed, the quick turn to embarrassed indignation, to entitled anger. To: I think my bedpan needs emptying, to something ugly muttered under the breath.

Home not being much of a safe haven. She'd stepped off the boat and into the home of her sister and her sister's husband, a guest (she thought) whose chores and responsibilities quickly began to feel more like payment. Her older sister, Angela, perhaps envious of her younger sister's looks. How angry Angela had been when she'd borrowed Angela's sweater, how her brother-in-law had looked at her in her sweater, how Angela pretended not to notice. Could draw a line from that moment to the moment, not three months later, when she found herself kicked out of the house, sent packing to live with a different sister in Ohio. How Angela packed her suitcase for her, bought a one-way bus ticket to Akron.

(A few months later, Dorothy gets a letter. From her sister Angela. She opens it, curious. Inside is a bill, itemized, for the twelve weeks that Dorothy lived with her sister. Ten cents: bowl of rice. Fifteen cents: long shower surcharge. Twenty cents: laundry. Included in the bill is the price of Dorothy's bus ticket.)

INT. GREYHOUND BUS—AMERICAN BACKROADS—DAY

Dorothy rides the bus through miles of

highways, perhaps nondescript to some, but to her, this is grandeur. The countryside she pictured, in the country she long imagined. The panoramic scenery, the flatness of the landscape, the rivers and lakes, the gray and blue and silver and pink skies.

It's enough to keep her occupied, to keep her mind off of the looks from fellow passengers, from the men at the truck stops where they take bathroom and meal breaks. Enough to help her ignore the smell on the bus, four days in early summer crammed in with fifty-eight strangers. It's the smell of people, and she can work with that. She is going north, to Ohio, and she can work with that, too, moving across the map in her head, like in a movie, her vector of travel a dashed line visibly inching across a map of the continent.

To add injury to the insult of having been kicked out by Angela, Dorothy realizes that her sister has kept all but one of her books (no doubt as collateral for the asserted debt). The sole book now in Dorothy's possession is a copy of Hamilton's *Mythology*. A book she has loved since childhood, when she spied the tattered paperback in a bin in her local library, passed over by all the other kids for its ruined state. It says on the back, published in the U.S.A. She has learned to read this foreign language from this book, this book of myths. She loves each of the little chapters, how they are short, and self-contained, but also all fit together in a

larger universe of gods and goddesses,
spirits, lower and higher, deities of all
types and their seconds, their assistants,
their rivalries and hierarchies, their
relative powers and weaknesses. Their petty
squabbles and sordid doings and secret
crushes. Every time she opens the book, she
hopes to turn to a new page, a new god, a
little tiny thing. She likes the minor gods
the best, because they are easier to master,
to learn everything about. She can search out
and soak up all of the other things that other
people had written or said about this minor
god, and in that way become an authority on
such a god. And when she becomes an authority
someday, an expert in her own right, she
thinks that maybe she might be able to make
her own entry in the book. To create a tiny
god from scratch. She has not named it yet.

Perhaps the god of bus rides. The god of
sponge baths, or maps, or minimum wage. The
god of immigrants.

INT. DOROTHY'S FUTURE

Flash-forward. Years later, the book turns up
again, in some generational story, of
immigrants and assimilation. Dorothy, now Old
Asian Woman, will rediscover the book of gods
(worn and destroyed by love and overuse, will
threaten to fall apart at any moment), will
read it to her son in their cramped one-room
home. Watch him puzzle over and struggle

through each word, his face an oscillating
pattern of consternation and joy, the delight
from the pronunciation of a word correctly,
the pure possibility in his way of reading.
The god of first times for everything. The
look on his face.

Years after that, Dorothy will get a phone
call. Her brother-in-law. Your sister needs
help. She will return to Alabama, and find
Angela sitting in the dark, in front of a
television turned to what appears to be a ten-
hour commercial. Angela is wearing a diaper
that has not been changed for a day and a
half. She has no food in her refrigerator and
no way to go purchase any.

Dorothy will clean her sister up, carry her
to bed. Make arrangements for her long-term
care, Angela's husband paying for it with
their savings. When the money runs out, and
her husband proves that he's not up to the
task, Dorothy will end up bringing Angela back
home with her. She will wipe and feed her
older sister for a year, two days shy of a
year, until Angela expires on a cool autumn
morning.

INT. GOLDEN PALACE CHINESE RESTAURANT

Ming-Chen Wu sits, listening.

                    DOROTHY
          So that's how I ended up here.

She realizes Wu is staring at her. Or gazing, more like gazing.

                    DOROTHY
          What about you?

Wu snaps out of it, embarrassed, tries to recover.

                    MING-CHEN WU
          What? Oh, sorry, I just—I like
          listening to you talk.

Dorothy suppresses a smile.

                    DOROTHY
          What's your story?

                    MING-CHEN WU
          My story? No, you don't want to hear
          it. Do you?

                    DOROTHY
          Yes I do. I really do.

EXT. MING-CHEN WU'S BACKSTORY

He's a few years older but his path is starkly different from hers. He was born into Historical Period Piece, the role given to him was Child Victim of Oppression.

BEGIN HISTORICAL NEWSREEL MONTAGE:

NEWS READER (V.O.)

On February 28, 1947, the ruling Nationalist Party, or Kuomintang, begins what comes to be known as the 2/28 Incident, a period of violent suppression of antigovernment protests. Over the next several weeks, tens of thousands of Taiwanese civilians are killed. *The New York Times* reports accounts of:

"indiscriminate killing and looting. For a time everyone seen on the streets was shot at, homes were broken into and occupants killed. In the poorer sections the streets were said to have been littered with dead. There were instances of beheadings and mutilation of bodies, and women were raped."

By the evening of March 4, Taiwan has been placed under martial law. An uprising of the people continues for a number of weeks after, with Taiwanese civilians controlling much of the island. Nevertheless, by the end of the month, the governor general of Taiwan, Chen Yi, bolstered by the arrival of troops from the mainland on March 8, has regained control. Chen Yi orders the imprisonment or execution of the leading organizers he could identify.

His men execute more than three thousand people.

In 1949, when Chiang Kai-shek and the Nationalists are finally and decisively driven from the mainland by Mao, Chiang and his loyalists flee to Taiwan, where they impose martial law again. This period begins on May 19, 1949. At the time it is lifted in the summer of 1987, thirty-eight years and fifty-seven days later, it is the longest period of martial law in the world. During this time, known as the "White Terror," thousands of Taiwanese are beaten, killed, or disappeared by the regime.

At the time of the 2/28 Incident, Young Wu is seven years old. He sees family members shot in front of him. He see his home and his town destroyed, looted, and set on fire. He sees men, and boys, not much older than he is, at first attempting to fight, and then attempting to live. He sees his father running back into his family home, which is on fire. Count to one hundred, his father says. And I'll be back here, safe and sound.

INT. GOLDEN PALACE CHINESE RESTAURANT

                    DOROTHY
          (interrupting)
     Why? Why would he do that?

INT. MING-CHEN WU'S BACKSTORY

He waits with his mother and younger siblings,
just babies then, for his father to come out.
He counts to one hundred. He pauses, unsure if
he should keep counting.
   When he reaches ninety-nine, he starts to
worry. At one hundred twenty-one, he starts to
cry. At one hundred eighty-nine, when he is
sure his father is dead, his father emerges
from the now completely blackened front of
their small house, carrying a box.
   Young Wu does not know what is in the box,
nor does he ask his father. He guesses his
mother knows, because she looks at the box,
and looks at Young Wu's father, and shakes her
head, as if to say, I can't believe you did
that, but also to say, I understand why you
did that.
   Later, Wu will learn what was inside the
box: a piece of paper. The deed to the family
plot of land. This land will be very valuable
in the future. His father risked burning to
death for his children's well-being, the
chance at a better life.
   But Wu doesn't know this at this moment.
What he knows is that the box is valuable,
because he just watched his father run into a
house on fire for it. Also watching were two
Nationalist soldiers, a private and a corporal,
who wait until Wu's father emerges, then calmly
shoot him through the back, the bullet exiting
from his throat. The box, along with the deed,
is casually scooped up by the corporal, and the

two walk off, leaving Wu's family there,
without a father, or a house, or a future.

INT. GOLDEN PALACE CHINESE RESTAURANT

Dorothy places a hand on Wu's shoulder. Lets
it rest there.

>   DOROTHY
>   You never knew him.

>   MING-CHEN WU
>   Not really, no. There are memories,
>   just a couple. Key scenes that replay
>   over and over. I was so young.
>   (then)
>   But I was the oldest son. I had to do
>   something.

>   DOROTHY
>   You came here.

Wu takes Dorothy's hand, holds it lightly.

INT. MING-CHEN WU'S BACKSTORY—JOURNEY TO
AMERICA

We see Young Wu, moving, in progress, making
his way to the new world. Bright-eyed, full of
hope.
   As a young student in Central Taiwan,
gazing at a map of the world in his classroom.

On the map, it is a jeweled blue, sandwiched between Canada (salmon pink) and Mexico (lime green). Young Wu dreams of the American air. Barbecues, baseball on the radio and in the streets.

In his dreams, he arrives on a bright Monday morning, the ship pulling into the port, friendly strangers waving him and the others onto shore.

INT. MING-CHEN WU'S BACKSTORY—THE UNITED STATES

In reality, Young Wu arrives in the dead of night. He waits in line to have some papers stamped, and then waits again in an area, sitting with fellow arrivals from seemingly every country on earth. It is cold, and except for the buzz of the fluorescent lights overhead, it is quiet. There is no one there to greet him. Once he is done here, he will get on a bus, where he will sit for the next four days, except for twice-daily stops to eat and use the restroom, and at the end of four days, he will arrive in Mississippi, where he will step off of the bus, in the dead of night, into a swarm of mosquitoes.

INT. MING-CHEN WU'S BACKSTORY—MISSISSIPPI—1965—DAY

He lives in a house with five other graduate

students, most of them from other countries. Nakamoto from Japan. Kim and Park from Korea. Singh, a Punjabi Sikh. And one more: Allen Chen, also from Taiwan. Young Wu wonders if he and Allen might be the first two people from Taiwan to ever live in Mississippi.

He will be paid a modest stipend to teach students at a university, and to begin graduate studies, to explore his own field. Young Wu's share of the rent is fourteen dollars per month. This is Mississippi, in a college town, in the 1960s. His graduate student stipend is one hundred dollars a month. The first time he sees the check, he thinks there has been a mistake. There has not been a mistake. Young Wu, for the first and only time in his life, feels rich.

On top of the hundred dollars per month, he receives a twenty-five-dollar allowance, once per quarter, for housing. One semester, he wins an award for being the best teaching assistant. Half of the class calls him Chinaman, but mostly they mean it affectionately. He is an overwhelming selection for the award. He receives a check for fifty dollars and a certificate. He makes a frame for the certificate, and sends the check home, as he does with almost all of his other checks. In general, he does well enough that he can afford to eat at a restaurant, once a month. He does not like hamburgers at first, but learns to ask for no mayonnaise or ketchup and eats the meat separately from the bun, lettuce, and tomato.

One day he comes home to find his roommate opening a can of cat food. Young Wu hadn't even known they had a cat in the house. He realizes they don't have a cat, that his friend, Allen Chen, is going to eat the cat food himself.

Young Wu takes the can from Allen, asks him not to do this ever again. Allen points to a whole bag of cat food he has just bought from the market in town. Young Wu says they will find a cat to give it to. He takes Allen to a diner and buys him a hamburger that night, and from then on leaves a couple of dollars on Allen's desk, or in his graduate department mail slot, every week. They look for a cat, together. Allen eventually finds one, and feeds the cat well, for a while.

When the food runs out, the cat keeps coming around, so they feed it leftovers.

All five of Young Wu's housemates are called names. They compare names. Chink, of course, and also slope, jap, nip, gook. Towelhead. Some names are specific, others are quite universal in their function and application. But the one that Wu can never quite get over was the original epithet: Chinaman, the one that seems, in a way, the most harmless, being that in a sense it is literally just a descriptor. China. Man. And yet in that simplicity, in the breadth of its use, it encapsulates so much. This is what you are. Always will be, to me, to us. Not one of us. This other thing.

But mostly the roommates are grad students,

and men, and they do what male grad students
do. They sit at the table, and smoke
cigarettes, pooling money to buy packs.

Young Wu will occasionally take a drag off
of Allen. They smoke, and drink watered-down
beer or cheap whiskey one of them has swiped
from a faculty reception. They laugh and play
cards and compare names they have been called,
mostly by the undergraduates. The faculty are
generally respectful, although for the most
part unmistakably distant. Some are even
reasonably warm. A few. The people in town are
the most varied. Many are polite, if silent.
Most are wary, with an edge of slightly
menacing disdain.

One day, Young Wu comes home in an
unusually good mood. Actually humming as he
walks into the house. The day is perfect,
jewel blue. Birds sing along. Young Wu sings
himself into the kitchen, where all of his
housemates were sitting at the table. He stops
singing when he sees the looks on their faces.

It's Allen.

What?

He's in the hospital. Someone beat him
unconscious. Called him a jap.

According to a witness, as the first man
hit Allen in the temple, knocking him to the
ground, they said, "This is for Pearl Harbor."

Young Wu thinks: it could have been him.
Nakamoto says: it should have been him.

All of the housemates realize: it was them.
All of them. That was the point. They are all
the same. All the same to the people who

struck Allen in the head until his eyes
swelled shut. All the same as they filled a
large sack with batteries and stones, and hit
Allen in the stomach with it until blood came
up from his throat. Allen was Wu and Park and
Kim and Nakamoto, and they were all Allen.
Japan, China, Taiwan, Korea, Vietnam.
Whatever. Anywhere over there. Slope. Jap.
Nip. Chink. Towelhead. Whatever. All of them
in the house, after that, they should become
closer. But they don't. They don't sit around
the table anymore, comparing names. Because
now they know what they are. Will always be.

Asian Man.

More and more, they spend time in their
rooms studying, or pretending to study. Lying
in bed, looking at the ceiling. Singh leaves
at the end of the year, transfers to Oregon
State. Park and Kim move out, share an
apartment on the other side of campus. Young
Wu loses track of the others quickly.
Eventually, as people do, they all lose track
of each other. Except for Allen.

He keeps in touch with Wu, writing letters,
which Wu returns, guiltily and belatedly,
about one for every three received.

Coming to enjoy, over the years, hearing of
Allen's exploits, as he climbs the ladder of
academia, then industry, as he turns out to be
the best and brightest of them all.

They never catch the three men who beat
Allen ninety-five percent of the way to dead.
Not that they need to be caught. Everyone
knows who did it. Allen goes on to star in

American Dream—Immigrant Success Story, that rare variation, the mythical promised land, someone leaving Chinatown for the suburbs. Living among the mainstream, which everyone knows means whites.

He goes on to get his doctorate at the Massachusetts Institute of Technology. He gets married, and has two children, a son and a daughter. He suffers headaches for the rest of his life, from the concussion he received in the beating. When he is fifty-one, he is granted a patent, which turns out to have a wide range of industrial applications, opening up whole new possibilities in several fields. The patent is acquired by General Electric for almost three million dollars. It's the first of several dozen patents Allen will go on to file.

Allen, newly rich, with a devoted wife and well-loved and loving children, decides to move out of his house for a while. He thinks about going back to Taiwan, but he had lost his immigration privileges and is afraid he will not be allowed back in if he leaves.

He does not feel at ease in the United States. Taiwan is not home anymore. Increasingly, he finds himself drifting back to Chinatown, where he's treated as a local celebrity. One of us, done good. Made it big. When Allen is fifty-eight years old, he takes half a bottle of sleeping pills and never wakes up. Two years later, Allen's daughter, Christine Chen, graduates from Stanford. Her mother and brother are at the graduation as Christine accepts the departmental citation in physics. She gives a short speech, in which she thanks her mother and her father. Her mother cries, and her brother claps. They all go out to dinner afterward. Two weeks after graduation, Christine is filling her car with gas at a rest stop off of the I-5. Someone yells out the window of a car moving at close to forty miles per hour that she should go back to where she came from, and throws a half-full beer bottle at her head. She is taken to the emergency room, where her scalp is sewn up with eleven stitches. She goes on to be a lead researcher at CERN, but like her father, suffers headaches for the rest of her life. She never visits Chinatown anymore.

Young Wu finishes his two years at Mississippi with a 3.94 grade point average. When he graduates, he is accepted in a doctoral program at UCLA.

Wu passes his qualifying exams at the end of his first year. Halfway through his second year, his mother falls ill, requiring him to drop out to earn money. He looks for work in his field.

In other fields. Willing to apply his skills. But there are few takers, despite his grades. After one particularly bad interview, the recruiter offers some unsolicited advice.

"No one really wants to hire you," he says. "It's your accent."

"I don't have an accent," Wu replies.

"Exactly. It's weird."

So Wu learns to do an accent, and then gets a job, the only one he can, as Young Asian Man, at Fortune Palace, a restaurant. Washing dishes, busing tables. In Chinatown.

He does the accent, learns how the place works. It is not who he is, but he learns how to be Young Asian Man, gets good at it.

EXT. DOROTHY'S BACKSTORY

She moves to Chinatown from Ohio, packs her one blue suitcase. She brings six blouses, four pairs of polyester pants. She brings a picture of her mother and father, standing up straight and about a foot apart, not touching, taken on the street in Taipei where they first met. They are both looking right into the camera.

She brings seven pairs of underwear, two pairs of shoes. She brings an anxious disposition. She brings a rowdy, somewhat unexpected laugh, the kind that erupts suddenly in a noisy party and then just as quickly disappears. She brings a memory of her mother dying in her bed at home, surrounded by her ten children, wondering aloud why, why, the question, undisguised. Why? Dorothy, throughout her life, will wonder now and then if that memory is trustworthy, or her own thoughts bleeding, over time, seepage from the frame into the picture.

She brings incense, and a shrine to her ancestors, and a smaller one for a particular, minor deity. The minor god of immigration and prosperity in real estate transactions. Which started out, a long time ago, as the greater spirit of irrigation and good fortune in agriculture. This is a deity who understands, above all: location, location, location.

To pray to the minor god, you close your eyes and you imagine a home for you and your family, with four bedrooms and two and a half baths, and you open your eyes and see yourself in southern California, and then you are.

But despite her prayers, people do not want to sell Dorothy and Wu a house. And that's okay, because they can't afford one. But people also do not want to rent them an apartment. Which would also be understandable, as Dorothy and Wu have a meager income, except that their income isn't the reason no one will rent to them. The reason no one will rent to them is the color of their skin, and although technically at this point in the story of America this reason for not renting to someone is illegal, the reality is, no one cares. The minor god of immigration has gotten Dorothy this far, but the real estate spirits have failed her. She and Wu rent in the only place they can go, which has the benefit of being a place they can afford. The Chinatown SRO.

They take the biggest room they can find, on the best floor (the eighth), in a room that is twelve feet by ten (half again as large as the standard ten by eight), their double incomes, as Young Asian Man and Pretty Asian

Hostess affording them a life of relative comfort, which is not saying much. But they can eat fish with most meals, and meat once a week, and they don't have to buy broken rice like many who live on the floors below.

They go downstairs together, working nights in the restaurant. She in the front of the house, he in the back. In her new job, she is scanned and studied, admired and assessed, pinched, grabbed, slapped, and, worst of all, caressed. The caressers fancy themselves to be gentlemen. They imagine that Dorothy returns their affections, plays coy or demure or even outraged, as part of the role. These gentlemen don't go for the quick palmful of buttock or breast, the momentary violation. Instead, they imagine a world where they could keep her, in some small apartment, and visit their little China doll.

Wu watches this, and bites his tongue. This is not the story. He is not a kung fu master yet, not supposed to defend her by taking out all these suckers with lightning strikes from his left foot. It takes great restraint, and constant reassurance from Dorothy, that he's doing the right thing, that they must do this to survive. Pretty Asian Hostess is what pays the bills for them, and he knows it, and that makes it even worse. In this place, Golden Palace, Dorothy is almost a star, the light hits her just so, focusing on the curve of her hip, the way the qipao fits her. This is what she is, and all she is, good for some eye candy while the businessmen talk to the crime bosses, the seedy underworld scene plays out. Sometimes she lives. Many nights, she dies. Opium, maybe, or a revenge killing. Some spurned lover. Or caught in the cross fire.

Sometimes she gets to weep before she dies, and on those nights, Wu will stop what he's doing, stand in the background, and watch her work. Watch everyone else watching her, too. Transfixed. And he'll know she's destined for more. She weeps, then she dies, then they go upstairs and wash up, celebrate by sharing a bowl of noodles with a few preserved radishes on top.

On off days, they venture out into Ext. Chinatown, not able to make it very far before they reach the end of the block, the area where the scenery ends. But it's enough, to get some fresh air, to see real daylight, to hear sounds without a soundtrack.

Dorothy tends toward those polyester bellbottoms and floral print blouses, with long, low, pointy collars. She pushes her midnight black hair back out of her face with a headband. She tries on looks, American woman looks, and with her fair complexion, she gets a kind of soft pass—begrudging admiration from the women, straight-up ogling from the men.

She isn't often called chink, although sometimes when she speaks, people have a hard time understanding her, or at least they pretend to have a hard time.

Young Wu has a harder time fitting in.

Wears pants an inch too short. Short-sleeved
shirts boxy and too big for his wiry frame.
They split a Coke, just like Dorothy used to
do with her whole family, and she drinks too
much and gets a stomachache, and he holds her
hand and lightly rubs her belly.

Young Wu turns to Dorothy and stops.

What is it?

We're going to get out of here.

At the end of the night, Young Wu has a
look in his eye, and this is the first time
Dorothy has ever seen that look on Young Wu's
face. The first time Dorothy had ever seen
that look on anyone's face. It scares her a
little. But it is also when she finally falls
for him.

                    MING-CHEN WU
          This is how we met. And fell in love.

                    DOROTHY
          In this place? This is no place for a
          romance. This is a place for the police
          to find dead bodies.
          This is a place where day and night are
          interchangeable, where we don't know
          who we are allowed to be, from one day
          to the next. How do we have a love
          story in a place like this?

                    MING-CHEN WU
          It's true. We don't choose our
          circumstances. We will have to fall in
          love when we can. Stolen moments.

> Between jobs, between scenes. Not a
> love story. But our story.

They're married in the restaurant, a small impromptu gathering of the waitstaff and cooks and busboys.

They luck out—two rock crabs get sent back to the kitchen, and a lobster comes back almost untouched, and they use every part of the crustaceans, frying up rice with the eggs, dicing up meat to eat with noodles. Someone turns on the radio. There's eating and dancing, and it's hot as hell, everyone sweating through their costumes, but no one cares tonight.

In the swirl of bodies, Wu takes Dorothy's hand, holds it lightly, whispers to her. *Not a love story*, he says. *Not our story. Just us together. More than enough.* She kisses him. A cheer goes up. Some large bottles of Tsingtao are procured, and it's a good time until they remember where they are. Who they are. The boss comes back to the kitchen and tells everyone to get back to work. Dorothy and Wu take a moment to collect themselves, and with heavy heads and limbs and full stomachs and hearts, put their Asian costumes back on.

GENERIC ASIAN KID

And then you arrive on the scene, Baby Willis.
A little tiny Kung Fu Boy. And for a moment
the backstories and fragments and scenes
filled with background players and nonspeaking
parts, it all makes a kind of sense, all of
it leading to this. A family. They bring you
home from the hospital, at which point
everything speeds up. It's a montage of first
moments, all of the major and minor
milestones: first step, first word, first time
sleeping through the night. There are a few
years in a family when, if everything goes
right, the parents aren't alone anymore,
they've been raising their own companion, the
kid who's going to make them less alone in the
world and for those years they are less alone.
It's a blur—dense, raucous, exhausting—
feelings and thoughts all jumbled together
into days and semesters, routines and first
times, rolling along, rambling along, summer
nights with all the windows open, lying on top
of the covers, and darkening autumn mornings
when no one wants to get out of bed, getting
ready, getting better at things, wins and
losses and days when it doesn't go anyone's
way at all, and then, just as chaos begins to
take some kind of shape, present itself not as
a random series of emergencies and things you
could have done better, the calendar, the
months and years and year after year, stacked
up in a messy pile starts to make sense, the
sweetness of it all, right at that moment, the

first times start turning into last times, as
in, last first day of school, last time he
crawls into bed with us, last time you'll all
sleep together like this, the three of you.
There are a few years when you make almost all
of your important memories. And then you spend
the next few decades reliving them.

GENERIC ASIAN FAMILY

You have done this before, all of it. Have
done your best to become Americans. Watched
the shows, listened to the tapes, eliminated
your accents. Dressed right, did your hair,
took golf lessons. Encouraged English at home,
even. You did everything that was asked of you
and more.

Your parents, they work. For the pleasure
of strangers, losing themselves in their
various guises. Saying the words, hitting the
marks, standing near the good light.

From the background, you watch.

At night, your mother puts on the costume.

At night, your father studies kung fu.

They weep, they die. They get by.

Finally, after years, he perfects it. He
emerges one day as a kung fu master.

He gets work as Sifu. He's in high demand.

You celebrate by frying up a steak, the
three of you eating happily and washing the
greasy meat down with a two-liter of Coke. A
toast: to not being other people anymore. Your
parents make plans to move from the SRO.
Everything is going well. Until it's not.

Until your father realizes that, despite it
all, the bigger check, the honorable title,
the status in the show, who he is. Fu Manchu.
Yellow Man. Everything has changed, nothing
has changed.

Yes, yes, your kung fu is perfect.
Immaculate, pristine, Platonically Ideal Kung
Fu from the highest plane of martial arts.

But, and we hate to ask this—can you still do the accent?

They ask him to put on silly hats. To cook chop suey, jump-kick vegetables into a thousand pieces. He hears a gong wherever he goes.

He is told: you are a legend.

You see where this is all headed, but it's too late. You can't control it. Neither can he.

Your mother weeps, and dies. Weeps and dies. Weeps and doesn't die. Just weeps. Because now, your father is no longer a person, no longer a human. Just some mystical Eastern force, some Wizened Chinaman. Her husband is gone, Wu is gone, even Young Asian Man is gone. They took him away from her. He is lost now, in his work, in who they made him. Distant. Cold, perfectionist. Inscrutable. No descriptors, anymore, no age or build, just a role, a name, a shell where he used to be. His features taken away and replaced by archetypes, even his face hollowing out.

This is how he became Sifu. This is how she lost her husband. How you lost your dad.

He comes in and out of the room, odd hours, waking you and your mother up to rant about this or that, to tell you his plans, how he will show them one day, to imagine a world in which his son can grow up proud to be in this family. He does this regularly if infrequently, then sporadically, then not at

all. You get news of him from others in the
building, hear rumors. He's taken to drinking,
breaking props. They put him in epics, and he
disappears for long stretches, just rumbling
drums and violent strings and always gongs,
always always gongs. They push in on his eyes,
the dead eyes, they've turned him into what
they wanted, what he was destined for all
along, a cheaper version of Bruce Lee. You
grow up like this, in Chinatown, your dad no
longer your dad. You can hear them talking at
night, about how to get out, about the dream
of getting out, about never getting out.

> YOUNG ASIAN MAN
> What happened? What have they done?
> They've trapped us.

> YOUNG ASIAN WOMAN
> Or maybe we did it to ourselves.

> YOUNG ASIAN MAN
> Were we always this? Wasn't there more?

> YOUNG ASIAN WOMAN
> There was. There can be more.

You hear them at night and you think: someday,
you'll get out.

EXT. THE ALLEY BEHIND THE RESTAURANT—PRESENT
DAY

First drag's the best drag. Second drag you
remember you hate smoking. You hold the
cigarette away from your body, watch the
lonely ribbon drift up toward the billboard,
thirty feet high in the sky:

                MILES TURNER   SARAH GREEN

                    BLACK AND WHITE

their perfect, huge faces, looking down on
you. Even out here, the light hits their faces
just right. Wherever they go that's where
they're meant to be, the center of things
always white and black and black and white.
Even in the picture, the tension is
unbearable, some spot halfway between their
two noses the romantic center of gravity, the
two of them facing each other, in profile.
Both of them with such luscious lips. Are
those their real lips? They can't be. You take
your thumb and index finger to your own lips,
checking to see how meaty they are. How do you
get lips like that? Lips that look permanently
ready to be kissed, a perpetual state of
plumpness. Supple. Pouty and tough. Those are
some sexy cops with sexy lips. You wish your
face was more—more, something. You don't know
what. Maybe not more. Less. Less flat. Less
delicate. More rugged. Your jawline more
defined. This face that feels like a mask,

that has never felt quite right on you. That reminds you, at odd times, and often after two to four drinks, that you're Asian. You are Asian! Your brain forgets sometimes. But then your face reminds you.

The door swings out, startling you. It's her. Karen Lee.

"Easy there," she says. "How's death?"

"Are you talking to me?" you ask her.

She looks around, as in, who else, dude?

"Sorry. I'm not used to, uh, women like you talking to guys like, uh . . . "

"Women like me?"

"Women with options."

She laughs. Studies you for a moment. "You're not really smoking, are you?"

You look at your cigarette. "No."

"Then why are you holding that?"

"I don't know. Goes with the outfit, I guess." You drop the cigarette, crush it out with your shoe.

"So. How are you?"

Whoa, you think. Is she messing with you? She's messing with you. She has to be messing with you. A woman like this is not going to be interested in a Dead Not Quite Kung Fu Guy. A Generic Asian Man. If there's one thing that you have to remember, it's that. Sure, they'll talk to you. Be your friend. But deep down, she doesn't think of you like that—

"Hey, Will, you still there? Lost in your internal monologue?"

"Sorry. I guess so."

"It's nice out, isn't it?"

"Yeah."

"Where are you from?"

"I'm from here. Chinatown. What about you?"

She flashes her eyes at you, and you almost die all over again. "Where do you think I'm from?" she asks.

"You want me to guess?

"I want to know your impression of me."

"Okay," you say. "I'll give it a shot: you went to a good-to-very-good liberal arts college in the Midwest. No—back east. You know how to ride a horse, drive stick, use chopsticks. You did a semester abroad in Osaka, yeah? Or Kyoto maybe.

Solid grades. You have an accounting degree to fall back on if your dreams don't work out."

"So far so good, except it was Taipei, not Osaka, history, not accounting, and I was dean's list all four years, and to be honest, I'm not sure what my dream is yet—it might be grad school—so I don't think I'll be crushed if, as you put it, it doesn't pan out for me."

"But that's the thing, Karen. For you, it always does. One way or another. Pretty Girl is never not going to be in demand. Kind of how it goes. Things work out pretty good for your kind. White People: Pretty Much Good, Pretty Much Always. Didn't they teach that in history?"

"I'm not White."

"White-ish. Close enough."

"Yeah. That's why I play Ethnically Ambiguous Woman Number One."

"You may have a point. So what . . . are you?"

"What am I? Nice, Willis."

"You know what I mean. Lee can be, you know, like Sara Lee, or General Lee. But it's actually, like, Lee. As in, Lee?"

"Lee, as in my paternal grandfather was from Taichung. He moved to the States and lived with us after my grandmother died."

"You're a quarter Taiwanese?"

"If you want to quantify it that way."

"Wow. Just—wow."

"What did you think I was?"

"I don't know. I thought maybe you were part Latina? Or maybe just came back from Hawaii and had a nice tan? Do you speak?"

"*E-hiau kong Tai-oan-oe.*"

"From your accent I can tell you speak better than I do."

"Do you need a moment?"

"This is very confusing for me."

"If you think it's confusing for you, imagine how I feel."

"Seems like it's worked out pretty well for you."

"I'm sure it seems that way."

"You're like a magical creature. A chameleon."

"Able to pass in any situation as may be required," she says. "I get it all. Brazilian, Filipina, Mediterranean, Eurasian. Or just a really tan White girl with exotic-looking eyes. Everywhere I go, people think I'm one of them. They want to claim me for their tribe."

"Must be amazing."

"Yeah, I mean, I can be objectified by men of all races."

"But you said it yourself. You can pass for anything."

"Seems like it'd be easier to be one thing."

"I'm one thing. An Asian Man. And that's all I am. Trust me, it's better to be you than me."

"Oh, boo hoo, I'm a poor helpless Asian Man. It's so terrible being me."

"I have to talk with an accent because no one can process what the hell to do with me. I've got the consciousness of a contemporary American. And the face of a Chinese farmer of five thousand years ago. Asian Man. It's a fact. Look it up. No one likes us."

"Not with that attitude they won't. And by the way, I think I might like you. Maybe. A little."

Wait, what?

LOVE STORY FOR A GENERIC ASIAN MAN???

No way.

LOVE STORY FOR A GENERIC ASIAN MAN???

For real?

LOVE STORY FOR A GENERIC ASIAN MAN???

They're rare, for your kind, but if you're lucky, in a lifetime, you might get one good one. Make it count.

LOVE STORY

You and Karen. The scene is set. Take your places. She's a tourist, you're a Delivery Guy. You can't stop looking at her.

BEGIN ROMANTIC MONTAGE

                    KAREN
         Oh.
         Are we starting already?

                    SPECIAL GUEST STAR
         And for some inexplicable reason, she
         likes you.

                    KAREN
         I guess we're starting.
         Why inexplicable?

                    SPECIAL GUEST STAR
         Because look at you.
         And look at me.

                    KAREN
         Why are we talking like this?

"Sorry," you say. "Force of habit."

"I don't want to practice dating, Will. I want to actually date."

"How do we do that?"

"You don't know how to date?"

"Not really," you say, looking down.

"Oh. Oh! I thought you were kidding," she says, realizing you are not. "Why don't we start with coffee?"

"I like coffee."

At coffee you ask her questions. What are her hopes, her fears? Where does she see herself in five years? She says those are bad questions. Those are questions if she were interviewing for a position at a law firm, not questions to ask on a date. You say right, right, as if you knew that, and then it is quiet for a second and she starts laughing and your face goes flush and you feel like you might have to run out of the coffee place but instead you start laughing at yourself and it feels so good. To have no idea what you are supposed to do or say and to be sitting across from this person who has just taken your hand and squeezed it then let go right away and then you're walking EXT. BOARDWALK—NIGHT, under the moonlight and she says, hey, how did we get here? You say moonlit strolls along the water are supposed to be romantic and she says this isn't a place, it's an idea, a generic romantic setting and you say well they don't call me Generic Asian Man for nothing and you laugh at yourself and this time it's easier and she laughs, too. This time instead of her making you laugh, you made her laugh and that feels good, making this person laugh, and you tell her that. She says she always thought you were funny. She'd worked with you before, and in the background you were always making cracks, whispering stuff to Fatty Choy or one of the other guys, little jokes under your breath, pretending that you were just trying to deliver a takeout order of Fried Rice Combo but then you accidentally witnessed several murders and that BLACK AND WHITE was really, at its heart, a show about the dangers of eating too much Chinese food.

You really noticed me? You want to ask her but you don't. You just let that fact sit with you— Karen Lee was aware of your existence before the two of you met. She saw you back there, not in the light, even when you weren't able to see yourself, and that fact changes everything. Now you're INT. CHINATOWN, sharing a bowl of tsuabing shaved ice with red bean and condensed milk and you're asking her questions about herself. You find out she has four younger brothers, the youngest of whom is in middle school. Her dad died when she was fifteen and her mom remarried. You like looking at her, it's true, seeing in her face, her features, little habits that you recognize, a Chinatown face, and also things that you don't, some threshold ratio of familiarity and difference, of comfort and newness, extending not just to the way she talks, the tones and rhythms of speech, but also thought, to the way she sees the world—from the background, from the margin. She may look like a future leading lady but she has the clear-eyed pragmatism of someone who started in bit parts. She takes care of people—her brothers, her mother—and you start to imagine ways that you could take care of her, care for the one who is always caring for others. You like how she is self-aware without being overly self-conscious, how she says what she means and does what she believes in. Your whole life you've wanted to be Kung Fu Guy, to be something you are not, and here is this person who is whatever she is at all times.

More coffee, more cold desserts. Talking. Some kissing happens. More talking. You play games. Would You Rather. Would you rather: be Handsome Dead Asian with no lines or Silly Oriental who says silly things? You do voices, slip into roles you've both done, share the dumbest things you've ever had to say at work. More tea, more eating of fried things, things on sticks, and laughing and taking on goofy roles. You want to tell her how you feel. You rehearse what you're going to say, imagine yourself in profile, dewy and tender-eyed. She notices you rehearsing.

"Will? What are you doing?"

"Being in love with you."

"No, you're not. You're falling in love."

"Same thing."

"Not the same thing," she says. "Falling in love is a story."

She says that telling a love story is

something one person does. Being in love takes both of them. Putting her on a pedestal is just a different way of being alone.

You try not to ruin this. She doesn't let you ruin it. It's going well. It keeps going well until the point where it normally stops going well and seems like it's going to start going less well, but then it gets to that point and it doesn't stop going well.

Karen sees you, talking to your mother. She approaches, smiling, nervous, sweet. A feeling rises up in you, a taste in your mouth, metallic, like fear. Karen and Old Asian Woman, meeting, in conversation. You can't imagine it. You can't imagine it so you can't let it happen. How do you stop this? Run away? Tackle her? Tackle your mom? But none of that's necessary. All that happens is you do a thing, small, a turn of your head.

"Oh," she says. "You don't want me to meet her."

"I do, it's just," you say. "She's not the easiest—"

"It's fine, Will. I get it." And she does. Karen doesn't let you ruin things. She understands your anxiety. She waits until you're ready for them to meet.

When you do introduce them, your mother doesn't say much. She smiles warmly, shakes her hand. Speaks some Taiwanese to her. Karen answers back. In Taiwanese. Karen says something about you that you don't quite understand. Your mom laughs. They both turn and look at you, smiling. What the hell is happening? This is not the way things are supposed to go. This is supposed to be when things fall apart but instead they are doing the opposite.

And then you stop being dead.

END ROMANTIC MONTAGE

BLACK AND WHITE
POST-DEATH
NOTICE OF REINSTATEMENT

RE: WILLIS WU

This is to confirm completion of the mandatory forty-five (45) day silent period following your most recent death event. You may now resume activities. Please note that by re-entering the system, you hereby acknowledge and agree to waive any and all status or other accumulated benefits you may have accrued pre-death. No continuity with any previous role will be recognized.

—CENTRAL CASTING

You share the news with Karen. This should be a good thing. For you to be back at work, with more purpose, more money to spend on dates. To save toward a future. You celebrate together over beer and noodles.

You start working again. Same shit jobs, but now you have confidence. Now you have Karen. You start doing better. Still bit parts, but the bits are slightly larger.

You climb the ladder. Again.

Generic Asian Man Number Three, Two, One.

Karen's career continues on its ascent as well—a higher, faster arc than yours. That doesn't bother you. You're happy for her. You are. You know she's destined for bigger things than you. Dating someone more successful than you comes with the territory of being who you are—there are more roles for Karen. Apples and oranges. Doesn't bother you in the least.

You see each other less. Twice a week becomes once, becomes once every other week. You talk but you don't.

"Hey."

"Hey."

"Where have you been?"

"Working."

"Okay."

"A lot."

"Do they not give you breaks?"

"I have to focus on my career."

You do. And Karen supports you. Her support

gives you even more confidence which leads to
even more work which leads to more
confidence. No more Generic—now you're a
guest star again. There's something about you
that's different. They can see it, whoever
they are that make these decisions. You've
got that intangible something now. That's
what they tell you. Guest star, guest star,
guest star, and then next thing you know,
you're recurring. You're on the verge of
something, a big break. You can feel it. And
then it happens for you. A meeting with the
director.

He tells you: All these years. Ever since
you were a boy. What have you dreamed of? He
tells you it's right there. You're so close.
Just keep working. Any day now.

You can't believe the news. Kung Fu Guy.
Any day now.

The plan is to share the news with Karen
over dinner. But then she shares her news
first. A baby.

"A what?" you say.

"A baby. You know, one of those small
humans. You're not happy?"

"Of course I am," you say. "It's just, I
don't know. I can't see myself that way. I'm a
Special Guest Star. I'm doing better than I
ever have, but I still don't make enough to
support a family."

"News flash. I'm doing pretty well myself."

"Oh I know you are."

"I don't know what that means, and we
should talk about that later. But for now, I

just want to ask, why are you ruining this moment, Willis?"

"Oh my God," you say. You are ruining this moment. You're an idiot. "I'm so sorry." You kiss Karen's face and neck and face again, you hold her tight then get worried you're holding her too tight. You take out your stash of envelopes and make a decent pile of tens and twenties and you buy a tiny ring and you get down on one knee and you ask her to marry you. She says yes.

The two of you get married at the courthouse. You have a new resolve, throwing yourself into work. She wonders aloud where you'll all live. Chinatown? In the SRO?

A month. Two months. A trimester. Another. Then one more. Then:

You're parents.

You hold your daughter in your arms. She looks at you and you know that she came from somewhere else, somewhere beyond your comprehension, the little tiny interior space you've been living in, inside your own dumb head. You know she is an alien from another planet here to save you. A being from some faraway land. She takes one look at you and you know that she knows things about you and you know things about yourself that you didn't before. You have been a father for approximately ten seconds and you know for certain that you will never be the same.

You and Karen name her Phoebe.

Karen and Phoebe and you, in the SRO. You can't raise this kid here, you think. But for

the time being, until you make it, it'll have
to do. All of you in the room on eight. Cozy.
Noisy. The sounds of the building traveling up
the central column. Hot garbage wafting up in
thermal waves. The baby crying through the
night, the neighbors banging on your floor and
ceiling. You do the cop show. As Ethnic
Recurring. The hours are longer but the
envelopes are fatter. You are on the verge.
Again. Like you have been for a while.

You come home one day and Karen's making
noises at the baby. The evening switch-off—she
hands the baby to you, gets ready to go to
her job now.

"I have big news," she says, her back
turned, getting dressed for work. She's
uncharacteristically nervous. You can hear it
in her voice.

"Okay," you say, "let's hear it." You don't
know why you said it like that. That starts
things off on the wrong note already. Karen
knows this is going to be weird, and on some
level, so do you.

"My own show," she says. "A huge role. I'm
playing a young mother." For once it's about
her, as it should be. Breathless, it all comes
tumbling out, the responsibility, how
important the role is, the anchor of the
story. She can't contain herself.

"There's even a part for you in it," she
says. "We can move out of here. Start a new
life."

You smile, your face tight. Bounce the baby
gently. Look at her little face.

"Willis," she says. "What do you think?"

"It's great. It's great."

"I know it is. But the fact that you said it like that makes me think you don't think it is."

"It's great."

"I don't get it. Isn't this what you wanted? To move out of here?"

"Yeah. I mean, yeah."

"But you wanted to be the one who did it. Is that it? You wanted to be the one who moved us out."

"I'm really close to making it, Karen."

"You've been close for a while."

"You don't believe in me."

"I do believe in you. That's why I don't want to watch you do this anymore."

"You don't think I deserve it."

"Of course you deserve it. You've deserved it for a while. But do you really think they're going to give it to you? Today they say tomorrow. Tomorrow they'll say the next day. I just don't want you to be trapped. Like your father."

"Trapped? What do you know about my father? Do you even know who he was back in the day? You don't get to talk to me about my father. Or being trapped."

"I'm sorry. I'm just saying—"

"It's what's best for our family. I have to stay for now. I've worked too hard to get it. If I get this, I can provide for you, for our kid."

"We don't need you to provide. I can

provide. Didn't you hear me say I have my own show? It can be our show together."

"You just don't get it. I don't want to be on your show."

"You resent me. For doing better—"

"Say it. For doing better than I have. But no, that's not it. It's not about you, Karen. It's about me. About becoming Kung Fu Guy."

"Seriously? It's still about that? After all this time?"

"What do you mean? Of course it is. This is the dream. This is what someone like me has available to him. Of course it's still about that."

"There are other things worth pursuing, Willis. The world is out there, and it's big."

"Maybe not for me. I'm sorry, okay? I'm sorry I can't let go of this yet."

"So what are you saying? You don't want to be part of this family?"

"I do. I do, Karen. We can make it work. Like I said, I'm close to getting everything I've worked for, and as soon as I do, things will change. I'll come join your show, but with my own thing. I just need to do this."

"The show's set in the suburbs. Deep. Nowhere near here. Long-distance doesn't work with a kid, Willis."

"Just for a while. A few weeks. Maybe a couple of months."

"A couple of months?"

"Tops."

So she goes. And I keep working. A few weeks turns into a couple of months which turn into several. Several months turns into a year. More. That creeping feeling. Karen was right. Something you've known all along, maybe. It's never going to happen. You should quit now.

A glimmer. A glimpse of a life outside this. And then, perfect timing, right when you start to seriously consider for the first time in your life an existence outside of Chinatown, the phone rings and it's the director and he says the words you have been waiting to hear all your life.

Congratulations.

You are:

KUNG FU GUY

No Karen here to share the moment. You're alone. You got exactly what you wanted. Didn't you? Or did they give it to you. The thing you thought you wanted. The role of a lifetime is one you can never bring yourself to quit. Karen was right: you are trapped. Doing well *is* the trap. A different kind, but still a trap. Because you're still in a show that doesn't have a role for you.

INT. GOLDEN PALACE CHINESE RESTAURANT

You're standing by the food table. It's this table of food. You can eat the food. No one's counting. But you also don't want to embarrass yourself. It's easy to embarrass yourself. They have everything: little finger sandwiches

cut into triangles or squares, roast beef or
smoked turkey or cucumber tomato for the
vegetarians or pretend vegetarians, heaping
mounds of curry chicken salad and shrimp salad
and tarragon pasta salad, all kinds of foods
in stick form, carrot sticks, celery sticks,
zucchini sticks, cubes of cheese (three
colors, although to be honest you can't tell
the difference), and that's not even getting
into the desserts. Pyramids of brownies and
blondies and dainty miniature red velvet
cupcakes and vegan versions of all of the
above. Snickerdoodles as big as your head.
Candy, gum, mints, coffee, tea, soda.
Sometimes if the day goes long, they'll bring
out a surprise: Korean tacos stuffed with
bulgogi and kimchi slaw. Handmade ice cream
sandwiches. You're standing there, stuffing
greasy cold cuts into napkins, sneaking
balled-up meat bombs into the pockets of your
kung fu pants, a meal that you can sneak back
at the end of the day. You stop to consider
what you are doing. Still playing a part that
was handed to you, written for Asian Man. You
understand: you've made a mistake. The biggest
mistake of your life. Man. You screwed up. You
need to go find your family. How do you get
out? You can't go out the front door. You
sneak out the back.

EXT. ALLEY

You look up at the billboard. BLACK and WHITE.

You can't be a part of this anymore. Their car is parked there. A getaway car for you—now on the run. You jimmy the lock, hotwire the ignition, and you're off. Driving off. Behind you, you hear sirens. You step on the gas and lose them.

Local Chinese children were
also dressed as rural
peasants by day to add to
the ambience. By night they
changed back into their
normal Western clothes.

Bonnie Tsui

When . . . an outsider
happens upon a performance
that was
not meant for him . . .
the performers will find
themselves temporarily
torn between two possible
realities.

Erving Goffman

ACT V
KUNG FU DAD

INT. CHILD'S BEDROOM—MORNING

Upbeat music jangles and jumps!

> SINGING CHILDREN
> We're up, we're up, we're happy.

Phoebe Wu sits up in bed, stretches her arms,
her yawning mouth a perfect O.

> SINGING CHILDREN (CONT'D)
> Rise and shine, Phoebe Wu!

INT. BATHROOM—MORNING—MOMENTS LATER

Phoebe, now dressed, brushing her teeth,
singing along.

INT. KITCHEN—MORNING—A LITTLE LATER

Phoebe enters the kitchen, singing.

> PHOEBE
> (singing)
> *Xie Xie Mei Mei!*

> SINGING CHILDREN
> (echoing)
> *Xie Xie Mei Mei!*

> PHOEBE
> *Bu iong xie!*

Phoebe, backpack on now, lines up with
children of identical heights, large heads and
tiny bodies, bobbing along.

Singing children. Phoebe joins, in step, in
key, as they file into the bus, heads bobbing,
off to school:

> Singing Children
> *Xie Xie Mei Mei!*
> *Xie Xie Mei Mei!*

It's a cartoon. Sort of.
Real people against an animated backdrop, a
show about a little Chinese girl, Mei Mei
(little sister), and her adventures in a new
country.
The country is geographically unique and
logically impossible, some amalgam of dynastic
China, a Taiwanese village in the olden days
(before imperial colonizers!), and some focus-
group-tested, aesthetically engineered,
perfect mythical U.S. suburb. Location,
location, location, three of them, composited
into one perfect synthesis incorporated and
flattening, the world as a children's
illustrated atlas, primary colors and rounded
edges, smoothing out the map, blurring the
boundaries and natural barriers, an optimistic
amnesiac's retelling of the age-old story of
immigration, acculturation, assimilation.

Mei Mei can move freely between these
places, just by stepping through a doorway,

into the next room. Space and time, apparently, being highly malleable, as Mei Mei navigates her new country, learning words for foods, and places, questions ("Where is the bathroom?" and "How much are the squash?"), directions ("Turn left for the police station, turn right for the bank").

Strangers are friendly, for the most part, and why not, given Mei Mei's pink-cheeked post-toddler disposition, precocious for a five-year-old but still innocent enough to not have encountered anyone at school who might make fun of her short-sleeved flowered silk shirt, or, even more likely, recoil at the smell of the fermented black beans in the lunch box her a-kong packed for her.

Xie Xie Mei Mei, you sing.

Xie Xie Mei Mei, the other kids sing.

INT. PHOEBE'S ROOM—MORNING

Phoebe opens the door to see you standing there.

> PHOEBE
>
> Daddy!

> KUNG FU DAD
>
> Phoebe.

> PHOEBE
>
> I haven't seen you in so long.

                    KUNG FU DAD
          I know. I'm sorry.

                    PHOEBE
          I asked Mom why we couldn't visit. She
          said you were busy.

                    KUNG FU DAD
          I missed you.
             (looking around)
          This place is not how I imagined it.

She jumps into you for a quick hug.

                    KUNG FU DAD
          Oof. You got heavy.
             (then)
          Where did the years go?

                    KAREN (O.S.)
          Nice of you to drop by, Will.

Karen appears in the window.

                    KUNG FU DAD
          Karen—wow, holy shit, you look great.
          Like really great.

                    PHOEBE
          Oops Daddy! You said a grown-up word!

          SINGING CHILDREN (O.S.)
          He said a grown-up word!

                    KUNG FU DAD
Sorry.
          (to the children)
I shouldn't have said that.

                    KAREN
Nice of you to say, Will, although
fairly inappropriate on all fronts.

Phoebe is leading the singing children in a
single-file line, getting ready for the next
segment.

                    KUNG FU DAD
          (re: Phoebe)
She's, like, a person now. When did she
get so big?

                    KAREN
Time flies when you're doing the kid
show.

                    KUNG FU DAD
It's a lot to process. I just learned
that my daughter is this amazing person.

                    KAREN
We're all learning a lot. But mostly
just you. Speaking of which:
          (leads children in song)
And now it's learning time!

                    KUNG FU DAD
I don't want to sing.

KAREN

Learning time is a special time,
learning time is—

KUNG FU DAD

No, seriously.

KAREN

Learning is a serious matter. Try to
keep up. You'll figure it out.

PHOEBE

So, what are we going to learn about
today?

KUNG FU DAD

I . . . don't know. I guess I could
show you some kung fu moves?

Phoebe laughs. Karen looks concerned.

PHOEBE

Haha, Daddy is silly, isn't he?

KAREN
(deadpan)
He sure is. A silly, silly man.

PHOEBE

I like kung fu. But we usually save
physical activity for our Move Your
Body segment!

KAREN

This is the part where we learn songs

and rhymes with positive messages about
tolerance and inclusion!

                    CHILDREN (O.S.)
Yay!

                    PHOEBE
And culture and food and vocabulary!

                    CHILDREN (O.S.)
Yay! Yay! Yay!

                    KUNG FU DAD
Tell me one thing. In this story, are
we together?

                    KAREN
No, Will. That was your choice.

                    PHOEBE
Divorce is a part of life!

                    KUNG FU DAD
    (to Karen)
They talk about divorce on this show?

                    KAREN
You need to watch more kids' shows.

                    PHOEBE
I have two parents and they love me
just as much. Now I have two homes
instead of one.

                    CHILDREN (O.S.)
          Sometimes grown-ups need to make hard
          choices!

                         KAREN
          Maybe we should talk. Privately.

                      KUNG FU DAD
          Is there somewhere we can go?

INT. PHOEBE LAND—GROWN-UP TALKING PLACE

You peek out the window. All clear.

                         KAREN
          You just show up here? After all this
          time?

                      KUNG FU DAD
          I missed you. I mean her. Phoebe.
             (re: Phoebe Land)
          How did this happen?

                         KAREN
          You said you didn't want her to grow up
          in the SRO.

                      KUNG FU DAD
          But. This place?

                         KAREN
          You lost the right to make that decision.

(then)
I'm going to leave you to get to know
your daughter now. If you take her
outside to play, make sure to put
sunscreen on her.

A muffled whimper out of Phoebe. She does this
thing, when she gets nervous, a tiny clearing
of her throat, almost a squeak, usually twice,
maybe four times, always in twos. Self-
comforting. You look over at your daughter.

                    KUNG FU DAD
          Didn't realize you were there, honey.

                    PHOEBE
          It's okay.

                    KUNG FU DAD
          Also, sorry for being a, uh, crappy
          dad.

                    PHOEBE
          It's fine. You tried.

                    KUNG FU DAD
          Do you want to play something?

                    PHOEBE
          We need to retreat to the castle!

Phoebe runs off, the sobs trailing after her
now, bursting into full-fledged running and
crying.

                    KUNG FU DAD
        The castle?

INT. CASTLE (AKA PHOEBE'S CLOSET)—DAY

You follow the sound of her talking to
herself, climbing up a tower, the winding
staircase narrowing as it ascends, until you
come to a door just big enough for you to
crawl through.
   The door is ajar, and from the room inside,
you catch Phoebe, mid-story.

                    PHOEBE
            (softly, to herself)
        . . . and I'll have a store where I
        sell things I make. I will make a comic
        book and I am going to sell it, and if
        I make something else, I will sell it,
        too. I will sell things for a dollar or
        a hundred dollars but if you have no
        money I will sell things to you for a
        penny and you can give me the penny
        whenever or you don't have to give me a
        penny, I will sell it to you for no
        money and I will give you a hundred
        dollars. Daddy said he will help me
        with the store . . .

She pauses, for a breath.

                    PHOEBE (CONT'D)
        He is busy working right now but he is

smart and tall and when he is done
working on the weekend we will work on
setting up the store. Also at the store
we will sell stuffed animals and if you
buy a stuffed animal we will donate the
proceeds to help animals that get
killed for their tusks and horns like
elephants and rhinos . . .

Watching her is like finding old letters, of
things you knew thirty years ago and haven't
thought of since. How to feel, how to be
yourself. Not how to perform or act. How to be.

You survey the room: drawings, hair ties,
notes to herself. Seemingly every species of
stuffed animal or creature, real or imagined,
lined up like a royal court along the walls on
the floors. Her friends, her audience. Her
off-screen voices. She seems both more
resourceful and yet more childlike at the same
time—how she's invented a world, stylized, so
that its roles and scenery, its characters and
rules, its truths and dangers, all fit within
one room. How small it is, and overstuffed,
and ready for expansion. How bright it is, how
messy. This whole place, the objects in it,
all from her.

                    KUNG FU DAD
          You made all of this.

                       PHOEBE
          (shy)

Yeah.

> KUNG FU DAD
> How did you do it?

> PHOEBE
> Do what?

> KUNG FU DAD
> Build a castle. Build a whole world.

> PHOEBE
> Oh. Like this.

She shows you, using what she has. Small
rounded kid scissors. Scraps of fabric. Glue,
tape, a binder clip, some string. Strips of
paper on which she labels her world, names for
everything written carefully in neat cursive
that wanders around the page.

She pauses. She's a thoughtful kid.
Already better at this than you are. You
can already see the day when you'll have
aged into your next role, when you'll put
on the old-man suit. You'll fumble, feeling
the future slip away, and she'll still be
young, moving away from you with every
moment.

> PHOEBE
> The thing about building a castle in
> the air is it's easy. You build up.
> It's like a little ladder, then you
> start building a castle in the air.

Then, you destroy the ladder. And your
castle is floating.

KUNG FU DAD
Why do you need the ladder in the first
place?

PHOEBE
Dad!

KUNG FU DAD
Sorry. Is that a dumb question?

PHOEBE
There are no dumb questions.

CHILDREN (O.S.)
There are no dumb questions!

KUNG FU DAD
Thanks honey. And thanks, weird
children that I am unable to see.

PHOEBE
You can't just build in the air.

KUNG FU DAD
Right. Of course.

PHOEBE
It's not connected to anything. So you
build a bridge to the air, then you can
break that bridge. But nothing falls
down.

                    KUNG FU DAD
      Makes sense. That's cool.

                    PHOEBE
      See, this is a big pig face I built in
      the air. It's a huge head of a huge
      pig and it's huge.

                    KUNG FU DAD
      I like that.

Phoebe smiles. Then frowns.

                    PHOEBE
      Okay, I'm done with this. I want to
      draw now.

                    KUNG FU DAD
      I'll watch you draw.

                    PHOEBE
      I don't feel like drawing anymore. I
      just want to sit with you here.

                    KUNG FU DAD
      That's okay, too.

The words coming out of your mouth, you can
feel it happening, how you're softening,
changing into a different person. You were a
bit player in the world of Black and White,
but here and now, in her world, you're
more. Not the star of the show, something
better.

The star's dad. Somehow you were lucky enough to end up in her story.

INT. PHOEBE'S ROOM—NIGHT

The truth is, she's a weirdo. Just like you were. Are. A glorious, perfectly weird weirdo. Like all kids before they forget how to be exactly how weird they really are. Into whatever they're into, pure. Before knowing. Before they learn from others how to act. Before they learn they are Asian, or Black, or Brown, or White. Before they learn about all the things they are and about all the things they will never be.

                    PHOEBE
          Wanna know what I'm afraid of?

                    KUNG FU DAD
          Sure.

                    PHOEBE
          I'm afraid of five things.

                    KUNG FU DAD
          Only five?

                    PHOEBE
          Five is a lot!

                    KUNG FU DAD
          Okay, let's hear them.

                    PHOEBE
Secret passages.

                    KUNG FU DAD
That's one.

                    PHOEBE
Waking up sweaty.
Getting eaten by a witch.

                    KUNG FU DAD
Two and three.

                    PHOEBE
A pebble flying into your eye.

                    KUNG FU DAD
That's a good one.

She pauses.

                    KUNG FU DAD
We're only up to four so far.

                    PHOEBE
I know.

                    KUNG FU DAD
What's five?

                    PHOEBE
I don't want to say.

                    KUNG FU DAD
        Why not? Just say it. I won't be mad.

                      PHOEBE
        Okay.
            (then)
        My dad dying.

                    KUNG FU DAD
        You don't have to worry. I'm very
        tough.

She looks at him, confused.

                      PHOEBE
        Everyone dies, Daddy. You live until
        you're one hundred. You turn one
        hundred and then you die.

                    KUNG FU DAD
        Let's go with that.

She seems satisfied. For the moment.

                      PHOEBE
        Can you tell me a story?

                    KUNG FU DAD
        I don't know how. No one's ever asked
        me to.

                      PHOEBE
        Can you try?

                    KUNG FU DAD
    Okay. I'll try.
        (deep breath)
    There once was a little girl who was—

You pause. Unsure of what to say next.

This is a key point in the story.

The next word, and whatever you say after
that, will determine a great many things
about it, will either open up the story,
like a key in a lock in a door to a palace
with however many rooms, too many to count,
and hallways and stairways and false walls
and secret passages, or the next word could
be a wall itself, two walls, closing in, it
could be limits on where the story could
go.

You search for the right word, the pressure
and expectation from her little face
mounting with each millisecond of silence
that passes, and it is about to come to
your lips and tongue, you are just about to
say it when your daughter turns to you and
says—

                    PHOEBE
    It's okay, Daddy.

                    KUNG FU DAD
    It is?

> PHOEBE
> Yeah. I can tell you don't want to right now.

> KUNG FU DAD
> No no, I have one. Here it goes.

> PHOEBE
> Wait!

She tucks herself tightly under her blanket, up to her neck, so she's just a head, two big blinking eyes. You study her features, see bits of yourself in there, but thank God, much more Karen.

> KUNG FU DAD
> Ready?

> PHOEBE
> Ready!

> KUNG FU DAD
> This is a story about a guy.

> PHOEBE
> I like where this is going.

> KUNG FU DAD
> This guy, something weird happened to him.

> PHOEBE
> Weird things happen to me all the time.

Yesterday, two of my toes got stuck
together for a whole minute.

                    KUNG FU DAD
That is weird.

                    PHOEBE
So weird.

                    KUNG FU DAD
Are they okay now?

                    PHOEBE
I unstuck them.

                    KUNG FU DAD
That's a relief.

                    PHOEBE
Dad?

                    KUNG FU DAD
Yes?

                    PHOEBE
I'm getting sleepy.

And then the children start singing softly,
an indistinct chorus of sounds, together
sounding like a lullaby. She falls asleep,
and you watch her for a minute, stroke her
cheek. When the sun is all the way down, you
rouse her for the nightly routine, following
the music cues, learning to be a parent on

the fly, out of necessity, winging it,
getting help from imaginary beings and
strange neighbors who are weirdly judgmental
but ultimately helpful. Your kung fu is
useless here.

Instead, this. A kind of dream. Her own
bedroom, her own bed. Her own yard. Without
a restaurant downstairs, or sirens or cops
or dead bodies. No fishy garbage fumes, or
flumes of mildewing vegetation, no cacophony
of five dialects being smashed together, a
solid block of sensory overload rising up
the dank central corridor of INT. CHINATOWN
SRO. Instead, phoebe land. This place,
without Generic Asian Men, unshaven, sweating
through their yellowing undershirts, no
Hostess/Prostitutes, no Old Asian People with
their weird breath and liver spots and
interminable wandering remembrances of the
old village and hardship and how they got
there. None of that. Just songs and flowers
and upbeat jangles and jumps. She lives
here, without history, unaware of all that
came before, and who are you to say that
this isn't the end point, this wasn't the
goal all along, that Chinese Railroad Worker
and Opium Den Dragon Lady and Kimono Girl
and Striving Immigrant and Honorable Dead
Asian Guy and Kung Fu Guy weren't all
leading to *Xie Xie Mei Mei*? To this dream of
assimilation, a dream finally realized, a
real American girl.

INT. PHOEBE'S ROOM—NIGHT

You do mealtime, you do bedtime. No kung fu.
Just spaghetti, and broccoli. PJs and story.
Brush. Floss. Pee. Glass of water. Feed your
fishes. Okay. Okay. Kiss kiss. Wait! What? You
didn't kiss the baby lion. Where is the baby
lion? I don't know. Oh come on. Here it is.
Okay, I kissed it. And the hamster dog. And
the hamster dog. All of them are kissed. Okay.
Night night. Stop talking. I'm not talking.
Stop whispering. Phoebe, really, no more. She
washes her face. Small, chubby hands, holding
the soap. Scrubbing her cheeks and forehead
with her soft baby hands. It looks familiar
and then you understand. That's how you do it.
She's been watching you. Learning. Brush.
Floss. Pee. Glass of water. Feed your fishes.
Kiss the baby lion. Kiss the hamster dog.
Kiss, kiss. Finally, after what feels like
months without a break, the moon comes out,
with its creepy but sweet moon face, the sun
closes its eyes and sinks down to the painted
horizon, and Phoebe, along with the rest of
Phoebe Land, goes to sleep.

INT. PHOEBE LAND—NIGHT

You lie awake, staring through a small open
window at a full blue moon, complete with a
silly face. This is the dream. Sustainable
employment. Some semblance of work-life
balance. Talk white. Not a lot. Get contact

lenses. Smile. They will assume you're smart. The less you say, the better. Try to project: Responsible, Harmless. An unthreatening amount of color sprinkled in. That's the dream, a dream of blending in. A dream of going from Generic Asian Man to just plain Generic Man. To settle down. To stay here. But you can't stay here forever. This isn't real. It's just another role. You can't, you can't, you can't. Can you?

You go to the window, peek out.

                    KAREN
          Is everything okay?

                    PHOEBE
          The police?

                    KUNG FU DAD
          Don't be scared. They're here for me.

                    PHOEBE
          I'm scared.

                    KUNG FU DAD
          I'm ready. I've been waiting for this.

The sirens stop. From a megaphone, a voice you recognize.

                    TURNER
          Come out with your hands up.

                    PHOEBE
Daddy no. No. No.

                    GREEN
Give yourself up and no one gets hurt.

                    PHOEBE
Are you going to jail, Daddy?
   (to Karen)
Is Daddy going to jail?

                    KAREN
No, sweetie. Daddy is going to prison.

                  KUNG FU DAD
It'll be okay honey. This is a good
thing.

                    PHOEBE
Prison is a good thing?

                CHILDREN (O.S.)
Prison is not usually a good thing!

                  KUNG FU DAD
In this case it is.

                    KAREN
I don't understand. How did they find
you here?

                  KUNG FU DAD
I might have stolen Turner's car.

KAREN

They tracked the vehicle.

She laughs. You laugh.

KAREN

You wanted them to find you.

KUNG FU DAD

I wanted them to find us.

EXHIBIT A
LAWS OF THE UNITED STATES

1859   *Oregon's constitution is revised: no "Chinaman" can own property in the state.*

1879   *California's constitution is revised: ownership of land is limited to aliens of "the white race or of African descent."*

1882   *On May 6, the U.S. (Federal) Chinese Exclusion Act is signed into law by President Chester A. Arthur, prohibiting all immigration of Chinese laborers, the first law preventing all members of a specific ethnic or national group from immigrating into the United States.*

1886   *Washington Territory's constitution bars aliens ineligible for citizenship from owning property.*

1890   *In the City of San Francisco, the*

Bingham Ordinance prohibits Chinese people (whether or not U.S. citizens) from either working or living in San Francisco, except in "a portion set apart for the location of all the Chinese," thereby creating a literal, legally defined ghetto.

1892 *The U.S. (Federal) Geary Act requires all Chinese residents of the United States to carry a permit, failure to carry such permit (at any time) being punishable by deportation or one year of hard labor. In addition, Chinese are not allowed to bear witness in court.*

1920 *The U.S. (Federal) Cable Act decrees that any American woman who marries "an alien ineligible for citizenship shall cease to be a citizen of the United States."*

1924 *U.S. (Federal) Immigration Act of 1924, also known as the Johnson-Reed Act, limits the number of immigrants allowed entry into the United States through a national origins quota. **It completely prohibits immigration from Asia.***

INT. COURTROOM

You're seated at the defendant's table,
wearing the only suit you own. The one you got
married in. Still fits, mostly.

Your lawyer walks in. It's Older Brother.

                    YOU
          Huh?

                    OLDER BROTHER
          Hey Will. You been working out?

You stand up, shake his hand. Older Brother
pulls you in for a hug.

                    YOU
          Where have you been?

                    OLDER BROTHER
          You serious?

                    YOU
          Yeah.

                    OLDER BROTHER
          Law school.

                    YOU
          Oh. Right.

                    OLDER BROTHER
          How is he?

                    YOU
Sifu?

                OLDER BROTHER
He need money?

                    YOU
Nah. I mean, yeah. But nah.

                OLDER BROTHER
All of those roles. He never got a
story.

                    YOU
You were the story. Supposed to be.

                OLDER BROTHER
I know that's what everyone wanted. A
kung fu hero. But I couldn't.

                    YOU
I think I'm starting to understand what
you mean.

                OLDER BROTHER
I never left. Not really. Not in the
way that counts—inside. In my mind.
Another part of me is in a different
place now. Interior Chinatown isn't
the whole world anymore. I had to
leave in my own way. Just like you
tried to do.

A door opens. Commotion in the gallery.

Lawyers shuffle papers. The judge enters the courtroom. Stares you down.

  Green and Turner in the first row, just behind you, ready to testify for the prosecution. The judge smiles at them.

                    BAILIFF
          All rise. Case No. 47311, *People vs.
          Wu*.
              (then)
          The Case of the Missing Asian.

                     YOU
          Hey.

                 OLDER BROTHER
          Yeah.

                     YOU
          Did you do well in law school?

                 OLDER BROTHER
          Really? Come on, Willis.
              (flashes a winning smile)
          I was editor-in-chief of the law
          review. Or did you forget who I am?

                    JUDGE
          The prosecution will call its first
          witness.

The assistant DA, brilliant and hard-charging and also has this incredible head of hair, auburn or chestnut, sexy in her crisp navy

pantsuit, looks like she stepped out of an ad
for navy pantsuits, rises, heads toward the
witness stand. Older Brother also rises.

> OLDER BROTHER
> Objection.

> JUDGE
> Objection to what?

> OLDER BROTHER
> Your Honor, we object to all of this.
> The whole thing. This mock trial. The
> entire justice system is rigged against
> my client.

> JUDGE
> Let me get this straight. Your
> objection, presented to the court and
> to me as its arbiter, is to the very
> legitimacy of the body you are
> presenting that objection to.

> OLDER BROTHER
> When you put it that way it does sound
> a little silly.

> PROSECUTION
> The prosecution rests, Your Honor.

> JUDGE
> You can't rest. You haven't presented
> your case yet.

PROSECUTION
Based on what's going on right now, we're
feeling pretty good about our chances.

JUDGE
Noted. Nevertheless, as a matter of
law, you have the burden of proof. You
need to present some kind of case.

PROSECUTION
Ugh. Fine. The prosecution calls Miles
Turner to the stand.

Turner is wearing a charcoal gray suit, very
faint pinstripes, cut for his build. He takes
the stand, clenches a couple of times. The
bailiff almost faints.

PROSECUTION (CONT'D)
State your name and rank.

TURNER
Detective Miles Turner.

His pec flexes under his shirt. Involuntary?
Maybe.

PROSECUTION
Detective, you've been investigating
the Case of the Missing Asian, correct?

TURNER
That's correct.

PROSECUTION

And in that time, you have had
opportunity to observe Mr. Wu.

TURNER

I've had opportunity to observe that
he's a punk.

OLDER BROTHER

Your Honor, come on.

JUDGE
(to Turner)
Detective, I'll caution you to keep
your comments professional and, more
important, relevant to the matter at
hand.

TURNER

Fine. He's not a punk. He's a weenie.

OLDER BROTHER

Objection.

PROSECUTION

Is that your only move? Let me guess,
you got an A in Objections at law
school.

OLDER BROTHER
(to judge)
I don't see how my client being a
weenie is relevant.

                    YOU
Can we stop referring to me as a weenie?

                  PROSECUTION
Your Honor, I will establish relevance.
If only defense counsel would stop
objecting.

                    JUDGE
Okay, I'll allow it. For now. But you
better get to the point, fast.
     (then)
That's a beautiful pantsuit.

                  PROSECUTION
     (giggles)
Thank you, Your Honor.

                 OLDER BROTHER
(under his breath) Uh oh.

                    YOU
Why did you say uh oh?

                  PROSECUTION
Now then, Detective, how is it
relevant, your observation of Mr. Wu's
character?

                   TURNER
He's internalized a sense of
inferiority. To White people,
obviously. But also to Black people.
Does he realize that?

A pause. Silence. All eyes in the courtroom turn to you.

                    TURNER
          He thinks he can't participate in this
          race dialogue, because Asians haven't
          been persecuted as much as Black people.
            (to you)
          Don't you need to take some
          responsibility for yourself? For the
          categories you put us in? Black and
          White? I mean, come on? Do you think
          you're the only one who's trapped?

Your cheeks flush, your foot starts twitching.

                    PROSECUTION
          Thank you, Detective. No further
          questions. Prosecution calls to the
          stand Detective Sarah Green.

Green takes the stand. The prosecutor makes
eyes at her.

                    GREEN
          Detective Sarah Green, with the
          Impossible Crimes Unit.

                    PROSECUTION
          Oh, I know who you are, Detective
          Green.

                    OLDER BROTHER
          Objection, Your Honor.

                    JUDGE
What now?

                 OLDER BROTHER
There's too much tension in the
courtroom. It's way too sexy in here.

                    JUDGE
That's a problem because?

                 OLDER BROTHER
For starters, it could influence
Detective Green's testimony.

The judge leans back, considers this.

                    JUDGE
Eh. I'll allow it.

                 OLDER BROTHER
     (to you)
We might be screwed.

                    YOU
I thought you were a good lawyer. You
should have stuck to kung fu.

                 PROSECUTION
Detective, I just have one question for
you.

                    GREEN
Go for it.

PROSECUTION
What are you doing for dinner tonight?

OLDER BROTHER
Okay, that's, that's, I don't even know
what's going on. I move for an
immediate mistrial.

JUDGE
Quit with the grandstanding. That stuff
only works on TV.

GREEN
Can I say something?

JUDGE
Of course you can. Anything you want.
Would you like to sit up here with me?
In the judge's chair?

OLDER BROTHER
That's definitely not allowed. This is
literally a sham.

GREEN
    (to you)
What are you looking for? Do you think
you're the only group to be invisible?
How about:
Older women
Older people in general
People that are overweight
People that don't conform to
conventional Western beauty standards

Black women
Women in general in the workplace
Are you sure you're not looking for
something that you feel entitled to?
Isn't this a kind of narcissism?
  (then)
Are you sure you're not asking to be
treated like a White man?

          OLDER BROTHER
He's asking to be treated like an
American. A real American. Because,
honestly, when you think American, what
color do you see? White? Black?
  (dramatic pause)
We've been here two hundred years. The
first Chinese came in 1815.
Germans and Dutch and Irish and
Italians who came at the turn of the
twentieth century. They're Americans.
  (points at himself)
Why doesn't this face register as
American?
Is it because we make the story too
complicated? Because we haven't figured
out how yet.
Whether it's a tragedy or a comedy or
something in between. If we haven't
cracked the code of what it's like to
be inside this face, then how can we
explain it to anyone else?

          PROSECUTION
Objection. Who cares?

                    JUDGE
Sustained.

                OLDER BROTHER
Can I ask a question then?

                    JUDGE
Go ahead.

                OLDER BROTHER
This is the Case of the Missing Asian,
right?

                    JUDGE
Yes. What's your point?

                OLDER BROTHER
If I was the Asian who disappeared, and
now I'm back and standing here and
obviously okay, and there is a clear
and plausible explanation for where I
was—at Harvard Law School—then what is
my client on trial for?

                 PROSECUTION
    (rises)
There was another guy who disappeared.

                OLDER BROTHER
Who?

                    JUDGE
    (points at you)
You.

                    YOU
I'm on trial for my own disappearance?

                OLDER BROTHER
Welcome to Black and White.

                    YOU
Am I the suspect? Or the victim?

                   JUDGE
That's what we're here to decide.
Prosecution may call its next witness.

                PROSECUTION
Prosecution rests, Your Honor.

Commotion in the courtroom. Ominous music.

                   JUDGE
Great. Moving right along. Defense will
call its first witness.

Older Brother looks at you.

                OLDER BROTHER
You ready for this?

                    YOU
I am. Also, do I really have a choice?

                OLDER BROTHER
You do know kung fu. And I can still
fight. We could just kick our way out
of here.

                    YOU
Let's call that Plan B.

                OLDER BROTHER
Defense calls to the stand
Mr. Willis Wu, aka Generic Asian Man
Number Three/Delivery Guy, aka Generic
Asian Man Number Two, aka Kung Fu Guy,
aka Kung Fu Dad.

As you walk across the room, you look out into
the gallery, which has tripled in size and is
now overflowing out into the hallway. It seems
like all of the SRO is in here now.

                OLDER BROTHER
State your name.

                    YOU
Willis Wu.

                OLDER BROTHER
Mr. Wu, is it true that you have an
internalized sense of inferiority?

                    YOU
What?

                OLDER BROTHER
That because on the one hand you, for
obvious reasons, have not been and can
never be fully assimilated into
mainstream, i.e., White America—

YOU
Dude, what are you saying?

OLDER BROTHER
And on the other hand neither do you
feel fully justified in claiming
solidarity with other historically and
currently oppressed groups. That while
your community's experience in the
United States has included racism on
the personal and the institutional
levels, including but not limited to:
immigration quotas, actual federal
legislation expressly excluding people
who look like you from entering the
country. Legislation that was in effect
for almost a century. Antimiscegenation
laws. Discriminatory housing policies.
Alien land laws and restrictive
covenants. Violation of civil liberties
including internment. That despite all
of that, you somehow feel that your
oppression, because it does not include
the original American sin—of slavery—
that it will never add up to something
equivalent. That the wrongs committed
against your ancestors are
incommensurate in magnitude with those
committed against Black people in
America. And whether or not that
quantification, whether accurate or
not, because of all of this you feel on
some level that you maybe can't even
quite verbalize, out of shame or

embarrassment, that the validity and volume of your complaints must be calibrated appropriately, must be in proportion to the aggregate suffering of your people.
    (then)
Your oppression is second-class.

                    YOU
Which side are you on?

                   JUDGE
It's a fair question, counselor.

                OLDER BROTHER
Your Honor, I'm building a defense for my client, based on his particular predicament.

                   JUDGE
What predicament is that?

                OLDER BROTHER
Someone who can't be viewed through either lens. Whose case cannot be properly considered by this court, where the rules and assumptions are based on a particular dialectic. Someone whose story will never fit into Black and White.
    (then)
The error in your reasoning is built right into the premise—using the Black experience as the model for the Asian

immigrant is necessarily going to lead to this. It's based on an analogy, on a comparison, on something quantitative.

But the experience of Asians in America isn't just a scaled-back or dialed-down version of the Black experience. Instead of co-opting someone else's experience or consciousness, he must define his own.
    (then)
I would draw the court's attention to the case of *People v. Hall*.

SUPREME COURT OF THE STATE OF CALIFORNIA (1854)

People v. Hall

Hugh C. Murray of the Cal S. Ct. ruled that the Act of April 16, 1850, Section 14, which forbade "Blacks and Indians" from testifying in favor of or against a white man, was applicable to the Chinese, who were legally Indians because both groups were descended from the same Asiatic ancestors.

From the opinion of California Supreme Court Justice H. C. Murray:

When Columbus first landed upon the shores of this continent . . .

he imagined that he had accomplished the

object of his expedition, and that the Island of San Salvador was one of those islands of the Chinese Sea lying near the extremity of India . . .

Acting upon the hypothesis, he gave to the Islanders the name Indian. From that time . . .

The American Indian and the Mongolian or Asiatic, were regarded as the same type of human species.

                    OLDER BROTHER
Murray's reasoning here is breathtaking in its twisted audacity. The legitimacy of categorizing "Asiatics" in such a way as to justify lumping them into the clause "Blacks and Indians" (in order to deny them the right to testify against Whites) is based on the subjective state of mind of a single man (Christopher Columbus) at a particular historical moment hundreds of years ago, who happened at that moment to be spectacularly and egregiously mistaken about where on the globe he had drifted into; thus a navigational misunderstanding of the world itself becomes the justification for a legally binding category.

                    JUDGE
Basically, a mistake.

OLDER BROTHER

Exactly. To put it another way, because in 1492 Columbus had no clue where he was, Chinese should have the same rights as Blacks, which is to say, no rights. Forget that this is likely a fiction—even taking the argument seriously on its face, the effect of this is that we have codified with the force of law a category: Blacks and Asiatics, separating them (because obviously, creating a new category of non-White), a secondary effect is that it also codifies Asiatics as outside the Black category. Inferior, and yet not in the same way Blacks were considered inferior.

The judge leans forward, listening now. Green and Turner, and even the prosecutor, too. Older Brother has their attention. Someone in the gallery yells, you tell 'em, OB.

JUDGE

Order. I'll have order in my court.

OLDER BROTHER

Somehow, in two hundred years, every wave, every new boatload of Asians, still as fresh, as alien to this land as the first.
(then)
This is it. The root of it all. The

real history of yellow people in
America. Two hundred years of being
perpetual foreigners.

Older Brother pauses. Takes a sip of water.
Not in a rush at all. Cool as ever. Your
heart, on the other hand, is pounding so hard
you think it might be visible through your
shirt. What is everyone thinking? How can he
be saying all of this, in open court, in front
of Black and White and the American justice
system? And yet—no one's kicked him out. Yet.

> OLDER BROTHER (CONT'D)
> They zoned us, kept us roped off from
> everyone else. Trapped us inside. Cut
> us off from our families, our history.
> So we made it our own place.
> Chinatown. A place for preservation and
> self-preservation.
> Give them what they feel is right, is
> safe. Make it fit their ideas of what
> is out there. Don't threaten them.
> Chinatown and indeed being Chinese is
> and always has been, from the very
> beginning, a construction, a
> performance of features, gestures,
> culture, and exoticism. An invention, a
> reinvention, a stylization.
> Figuring out the show, finding our
> place in it, which was the background,
> as scenery, as nonspeaking players.
> Figuring out what you're allowed to
> say. Above all, trying to never, ever

offend. To watch the mainstream, find
out what kind of fiction they are
telling themselves, find a bit part in
it. Be appealing and acceptable, be
what they want to see.
(then)
My client was a part of this system.
Both victim and suspect, he killed
countless Asian men.
(gasp from the gallery)
Killed them and then, six weeks later,
became them again, as if nothing had
happened, as if he had no memory or
remorse. He allowed it to happen,
allowed himself to become Generic, so
that no one could even tell what was
happening. He is guilty, Your Honor,
and ladies and gentlemen of the jury.
Guilty of wanting to be part of
something that never wanted him.
(beat)
The defense rests.

Silence. Then: applause. Hooting and
hollering from everyone. It's like the casino
and karaoke night and a party in the SRO all
at once—raucous laughter and unfiltered
emotion. Someone said it. Someone stood up
and said all the shit that we never say,
didn't even know how to say. Older Brother to
the rescue, after all, fulfilling his destiny
with his mouth and his brain instead of his
hands and feet.
    You look back to see if Sifu is in the

courtroom. You see Old Asian Woman. But you
don't see him. Where is he?

                    JUDGE
          The court will now recess while the
          jury deliberates.

The jury files out.

Green and Turner approach your table.

                    TURNER
              (to Older Brother)
          You should come work for the DA.

                    OLDER BROTHER
          Thanks. But I'm good.

                    GREEN
              (to you)
          Good luck, Willis.

When it's finally empty in the courtroom, you
turn to Older Brother.

                    YOU
          Wow.

                    OLDER BROTHER
          Are you happy with your representation?

                    YOU
          I mean, yeah. The way you talked about
          history and all that.

                    OLDER BROTHER
          You have no idea what I was saying, do
          you?

                         YOU
          Absolutely none. Seriously no clue.

Older Brother laughs. Nice to see him crack a
smile.

                    YOU (CONT'D)
          Just the fact that you stood up
          there, inside this building, in an
          American courtroom, and argued my
          case.

                    OLDER BROTHER
          Our case. I hope it was enough.

He goes out to the vending machine, buys you
each a soda.

                    OLDER BROTHER
          To our day in court.

You gulp down the can, just now realizing how
tense you are. Ears still buzzing, heart still
racing.

The jury's already coming back. Everyone
hurries back into the courtroom to hear the
verdict. The jurors file back in. The
foreperson steps up.

                    YOU
      (whispering)
That seemed quick.

              OLDER BROTHER
Yeah.

                    YOU
What does that mean?

              OLDER BROTHER
I don't know.

                    YOU
What does it usually mean?

              OLDER BROTHER
I don't think that's relevant. I've
never defended someone for self-
imprisonment before. Guess we'll find
out.

                  JUDGE
The forewoman will read the verdict.

                FOREWOMAN
Your Honor, in the case of *People vs.
Wu* aka Generic Asian Man, we the jury
of the people find the defendant:
Guilty as charged.

              OLDER BROTHER
This is bullshit.

The courtroom erupts into chaos. The judge
bangs his gavel to no avail. The bailiff has
his hand on his weapon.

                    JUDGE
          Order! Order! People! Settle down or I
          will find you all in contempt.
               (then, to you)
          Before I sentence you, do you have
          anything to say for yourself, Mr. Wu?

You look at Older Brother. He nods.

You rise, face the prosecutor, Turner and
Green, the judge, and, most important, all of
the assembled onlookers in the gallery. Up
front, all of you, on trial together. The
Generic Asian Men.

                    YOU
          Ever since I was a boy, I've dreamt of
          being Kung Fu Guy.
               (then)
          Man, my throat is dry again. I need
          water. Can I have water?

Turner comes over, hands you a bottle.

                    YOU
          Thanks.
               (you down the whole bottle)
          Ever since I was a boy, I've dreamt of
          being Kung Fu Guy. I practiced all
          those years, dreaming of tomorrow, of

the next day, of the day it would come. And then one day, finally, after waiting however many decades for it, after how many nights staring at the ceiling or my poster of Bruce Lee or hearing Sifu's words in my head, I finally got my shot. And when I did, you know what? I thought: I wonder why I wanted this so bad.

Murmurs from the gallery. The Generic Asian Men look confused. So do the Cheuks, and the Monk, and the Hostess, and the Emperor and all of the Asian Gangsters.

> TURNER
> They used you guys. Against us. Against yourselves.

Older Brother seems to understand, nodding along. Old Asian Woman, too—a twinkle in her eye. You finally got it. She sees it. You finally understood what she meant.

> YOU
> Kung Fu Guy is just another form of Generic Asian Man.

You've never really given a monologue before. The lights go down, except for the one on you. The light, it's on you, and it's hitting you just right.

> YOU (CONT'D)
> (deep breath)
> We're all the same. Aren't we? Generic
> Asian Man. Maybe I'm Kung Fu Guy at the
> moment, but I know as well as you all
> do that this is about half a rung above
> jack shit and I'm about one flubbed
> line from being busted back down to the
> background pool. It sucks being Generic
> Asian Man.

A couple of affirmative grunts.

> YOU (CONT'D)
> But at the same time, I'm guilty, too.
> Guilty of playing this role. Letting it
> define me. Internalizing the role so
> completely that I've lost track of
> where reality starts and the
> performance begins. And letting that
> define how I see other people. I'm as
> guilty of it as anyone. Fetishizing
> Black people and their coolness.
> Romanticizing White women. Wishing I
> were a White man. Putting myself into
> this category.

You find Karen's eyes in the gallery.

> YOU (CONT'D)
> By putting ourselves below everyone,
> we're building in a self-defense
> mechanism. Protecting against real
> engagement. By imagining that no one

wants us, that all others are so
different from us, we're privileging
our own point of view.
   (surveys crowd)
Look at all of you here. We got our
surfers there . . . our b-boys. Floppy-
haired emo guys. Clean fade lowered-car
guys. Tats, no tats. All of the
varieties of the Asian American male.
Most of us between five-six and five-
eleven. On some level . . . we do
share something. Played NES and D&D in
middle school. Our moms make the same
foods, frying up radish and taro cakes,
a dollop of hot stuff and a splash of
soy sauce. Snack time. Our houses smell
the same way, have the same
embarrassing piles of clutter, with
random-ass Asian shit mixed in with
plastic toys and free crap and a
mishmash of furniture and decor . . .

A couple of mm-hmms, guys climbing on board now.

                    YOU (CONT'D)
   . . . and bad carpet and so many
styles because it all equals no style,
because decor is not something our
parents care about or can afford.
Matching pillows and shit, that's for
White people. Our shit is functional,
like a table is where you eat and do
homework. And get good grades and be
well rounded in extracurriculars and

get into an Ivy or a good state school
and then you graduate with a solid GPA
and you come out here and find out that
what you are is . . . Asian Man. But
how often do you, or you, or any of us
ever think the thought, I'm an Asian
man? Almost never. Not until someone
reminds you. Some guy bumps you at a
bar, and makes a comment. Or you
overhear some people talking, and one
of them says, oh, your Asian friend so-
and-so. And in that moment, we all
become the same again. All of us
collapse into one, Generic Asian Man.
　　(then)
What I'm trying to say is, we aren't
Generic Asian Men. I mean, look at us.
We look ridiculous. All pretending to
be the same thing. We're not.
　　(pointing out guys in the crowd)
Choy, you know what I'm talking about.
Fong. And you, you definitely know what
I mean, right Carl?

                    NOT CARL
I'm not Carl.

                    YOU
Sorry. You get my point.

                    NOT CARL
I do. But I wish you knew my name. We
went to junior high together.

                         YOU
          I'm sorry, man. My point is, I'm
          looking out at all of you. And my
          parents, our elders, my friends.
             (then)
          At my daughter.

Old Asian Woman looks at you, then at Phoebe
and Karen.

                         YOU
          I'm looking at my wife. Ex-wife. But
          maybe ex-ex-wife?

Karen looks at you. She smiles. And frowns.
And smiles a little bit.

                       KAREN
          You're sort of losing the thread here,
          Will.

                         YOU
          Right. Thanks.

                       KAREN
          I love you, though.

                    YOU (CONT'D)
          And I just want to say one thing to
          all of you. The truth is, I am
          guilty. It's my fault. The question
          isn't where did the Asian guy
          disappear to?

The question is: why is the Asian guy always dead?

Because we don't fit. In the story. If someone showed you my picture on the street, how would you describe it?

You might say, an Asian fellow. Asian dude. Asian Man.

How many of you would say: that's an American?

What is it about an Asian Man that makes him so hard to assimilate?

Grunts from the gallery.

                    YOU (CONT'D)
Why doesn't he have a role in Black and White?

The question is:

Who gets to be an American? What does an American look like?

We're trapped as guest stars in a small ghetto on a very special episode. Minor characters locked into a story that doesn't quite know what to do with us. After two centuries here, why are we still not Americans? Why do we keep falling out of the story?

More grunts. Some mm-hmns. A "hell yeah."

                    YOU (CONT'D)
        I spent most of my life trapped.
        Interior Chinatown. I made it out, to
        become Kung Fu Dad. But that was just
        another role. A better role than I've
        ever had, but still a role. I can't just
        keep doing the same thing over and over
        again. My dad did that. And where did it
        get him? He was a true master, someone
        who had mastered his craft. And what did
        his life add up to? You never recognized
        him for what he could do. Who he was.
        You never allowed him a name.

        So what do we do?

You look at Older Brother.

The gallery is fired up now. Angry Asians. The
judge bangs his gavel, order order, but no
one's listening. It's about to explode.

                    OLDER BROTHER
        Plan B?

                    YOU
        Plan B.

The music kicks in. A dozen cops come busting
through the door, three from the front, one
from the back, and one from upstairs. You take
your stance. Older Brother next to you. Come

on, you say. Come get this. You fight off the
first wave, a bunch of slow-moving grunts, but
then another wave. Then another. The SWAT team
arrives. All the Generic Asian Men jump in now.
It's a melee. In all of the action, you find
it: the thing Sifu told you. One thing. One
thing a day. One thing at a time. Everything
slows down, the music fades away, and it's just
breathing. Your breathing, and the sound of
skin on skin, skin on bone, crunch and slap.
Your kung fu is free, is flowing, is at a
level it could never have reached, in all those
years. Up block, side step, body punch, side
kick, down block, down block. Jump, clear the
counter, push off, SPLITS IN THE AIR, kicking
two dudes at once, one in the face, one in the
throat, who did that? You can jump like this,
landing, no-look back kick, guy goes down with
a liquid-y sound, like he's a bag of organs,
the energy from your foot in a strike point,
radiating outward and who the hell are you, and
this is not B or B-plus or even A-minus kung
fu. Six feet above the ground, somersaults in
the air, butterfly kicks, twisting
horizontally, diagonally, three-sixty, seventy-
twenty, ten-eighty. Gravity can wait. You're
six again, you're fighting the whole world,
your mom down there on earth, you in the
clouds, Kung Fu Kid. You leap and twist, your
leg slicing through empty space, splitting the
world in two. Wave after wave after wave, until
you have nothing left, fighting with everything
in your heart and mind and body right up until
the very end, when you hear the gun go off.

INT. GOLDEN PALACE CHINESE RESTAURANT—NIGHT

Kung Fu Guy is dead.

                    GREEN
        He's dead.

                    TURNER
        Looks that way.

The Black cop and the White cop regard the
prone Asian male body, partially covered with
a sheet.
    A crime scene investigator swabs something.
Another one measures the radius and dispersal
pattern of a pool of drying blood.

                    GREEN
            (gazing at the dead Chinese)
        What are we looking at?

                    TURNER
        Family drama, probably. Some kind of
        cultural thing.

You open one eye, peek up at Black and White.
    "Hey," Turner says. Off-script.
    "I can't do this anymore," you say.
    Turner smiles. "Yeah, man. I know."
    "See you around, Wu," Green says, pulling
you up to your feet, a dead man now free.
"Maybe we can work together again in the
future."
    You close your eyes.

"Hey."

You open your eyes to see Karen leaning over you. Her hair smells so good. She kisses you.

"What now?" she says.

"Looking forward to hanging out with our kid."

Phoebe pounces, knocking the wind out of you.

"Did you win?" she asks.

"No," you say. "I lost."

"Are you dead?"

"Yes. No. I'm not sure."

"Who are you now? Are you still Kung Fu Guy?"

"Nope," you say. "I'm your dad."

"Kung Fu Dad?"

"Just dad."

"Oh," she says. "That's good." She pushes her head into you. Your side feels wet.

"Don't cry," you say.

"But I want to."

"Okay. Cry."

Black and White is leaving town. The cops all filing out. The place is a mess.

You see Old Asian Woman and Karen talking. Uh oh. They approach together.

"We were just talking," your mother says.

"This can't be good," you say.

Old Asian Woman turns to you. She makes that face. Secret pride, maybe. Or bittersweet pain. Little of both.

"You used to jump off the walls. Like a monkey." She asks, "What did you call yourself?"

"Kung Fu Kid," you say. Karen laughs. Old Asian Woman closes her eyes.

"You always tried so hard at everything, Willis," she says. "Maybe I was wrong," she says. "Telling you to be more."

"I just wanted you and Ba to be happy."

"I was happy. Eating dinner with you. Your chubby little hand, holding the bowl." You hug her, kiss the top of her head. It smells just like it used to. You are not Kung Fu Guy. You are Willis Wu, dad. Maybe husband. Your dad skills are B, B-plus on a good day. But you've been practicing. You say the words. Take what you can get. Try to build a life. Sometimes, things happen. Mostly they don't. Sometimes you get to talk. Mostly you don't. Life at the margins, made from bit pieces.

All the Old Asians, wandering, standing around. No show. No plot, no world. Just characters. Golden Palace dismantled. The sky up above. EXT. CHINATOWN.

POST-CREDITS

Miles Turner left the force to attend Harvard Medical School. He is now a surgeon.

Sarah Green started a singing career. She still moonlights as a PI.

Green and Turner have started seeing other people, but they're still friends. And sometimes more.

EXHIBIT B
LAWS OF THE UNITED STATES, PART II

1943   The Chinese Exclusion Act is repealed by the Magnuson Act and Chinese in the United States are given the right to become naturalized citizens, although ethnic Chinese in America were still prohibited from owning property or businesses. The quota for Chinese immigration is set at 105 people per year.

1965   The Immigration and Nationality Act (Hart-Celler Act) is passed by the 89th United States Congress and signed into law by President Lyndon B. Johnson. The law abolishes the quota-based National Origins Formula that had been the basis of U.S. immigration policy since 1921.

Chinatown, like the phoenix, rose from the ashes with a new facade, dreamed up by an American-born Chinese man, built by white architects, looking like a stage-set China that does not exist.

Philip Choy

ACT VII
EXT. CHINATOWN

MING-CHEN WU

Late one night you see him in the kitchen.
With Phoebe, both of them sitting on
overturned plastic crates, laughing. Wearing
one of his shirts from the seventies. So old
that it went out of style, came back, went out
again. On the verge of coming back around a
second time. He was, he is, more handsome than
you. In his eighth decade, enough thick,
black, straight hair to comb back and across,
a clean part on the left side. The way he
first learned how Americans did it, watching
old film reels in central Taiwan, his home now
a distant, watery memory from a Period Piece.
   This stranger, your father. Sifu still in
there. Flickering in and out. There is a
dusky, twilit understanding in his eyes—the
gulf inside that he is slowly falling into.
His eyes almost a little wet. The gulf between
the two of you. Permanent aliens to each
other. How many early mornings and late nights
has he spent there? Interior Golden Palace.
He's probably seen it reconfigured,
repurposed, same flimsy walls, a hundred
different stories, five hundred. Same small
space. This place preserved as if in amber.
Like a museum, a presentation of a time and
place that always exist, and never did. A
holding cell, purgatory, a vestibule, the
anteroom, the waiting room. It's in the United
States, but not quite America. Some trick of
geography. The story doesn't need to change,
doesn't need to evolve. Because it never

existed. Better if it doesn't. Dinner theater without a stage. Playing out the same tired old skit, chopsticks and dragons, Family and Duty, Father and Son. You wondered if it would ever change. You didn't know then what you know now.

Maybe, if you're lucky, she'll teach you. If she can move freely between worlds, why can't you? You watch him for a while. You want to reach out and touch his face. Then someone in the front of the house turns on the karaoke machine, testing testing.

"Dad," Phoebe says. "Are you okay?"

"Yes honey," you say. "Watch this. A-kong is up next."

Ming-Chen Wu takes the stage, smiles. Testing, testing, he says, and he clears his throat, ready to sing about home.

ACKNOWLEDGMENTS

This novel has the tremendous good fortune of being published by the many talented and hard-working people at Pantheon, Vintage, and the Knopf Double-day Publishing Group, including (but not limited to) the following individuals:

CAST

Cover Designer	Tyler Comrie
Text Designer	Anna Knighton
Production Editor	Kathleen Fridella
Copy Editor	Fred Chase
Proofreader	Chuck Thompson
Publicist	Rose Cronin-Jackman
Marketer	Julianne Clancy
Managing Editor	Altie Karper
Associate Managing Editor	Cat Courtade
Publisher Extraordinaire	Dan Frank
Fancy Pants Imprint	Pantheon Books

Like many indie productions, making this book was a labor of love. There were many moments of frustration and self-doubt. There were also moments of joy, of shared creation and discovery, thanks mostly to the intelligence and care of:

Executive Producer	Julie Barer
Executive Producer	Josefine Kals
Executive Producer	Anna Kaufman
Executive Producer	Tim O'Connell

Julie and Tim: this book would literally not exist without your patience, guidance, and extraordinary contributions. (And thanks as well to Nicole Cunningham at The Book Group.)

As evidenced by the epigraphs, certain books were invaluable resources to me in the writing of this novel (in addition to *The Presentation of Self in Everyday Life* by Erving Goffman, a book I will keep rereading until I can't read anymore):

American Chinatown	Bonnie Tsui
San Francisco Chinatown	Philip Choy

For generous financial support provided during the long, sometimes lean, years between books, I am grateful to:

Santa Monica Artist Fellowship	City of Santa Monica
Nathan Birnbaum	Cultural Affairs Director

There are certain other people whose support has been essential, both professionally and personally. Having the opportunity to work with people this smart is a privilege, but having them believe in me has been more important than they may realize:

Super Smarty Pants	Jason Richman
Super Smarty Pants	Mickey Berman
Super Smarty Pants	Mark Ceryak
Super Smarty Pants	David Levine
Super Smarty Pants	Katy Rozelle
Super Smarty Pants	Howie Sanders

The people whose lives and love inspire and motivate me to write:

Mom	Betty Lin Yu
Dad	Jin Yu
Daughter	Sophia Yu
Son	Dylan Yu
The Real Star of the Show	Michelle Jue

Charles Yu's first novel, *How to Live Safely in a Science Fictional Universe*, was a *New York Times* Notable Book and a *Time* magazine best book of the year. He was nominated for two Writers Guild of America Awards for his work on the HBO series, *Westworld*. His fiction and nonfiction have appeared in *The New Yorker*, *The New York Times*, *The Wall Street Journal*, and *Wired*.